Absent Love

European Women
Writers Series

Absent Love

A Chronicle (*Crónica del desamor*)

By Rosa Montero

Translated and with an introduction by

Cristina de la Torre and Diana Glad

University of Nebraska Press

Lincoln and London

Manufactured in the United States
of America
Originally published as
Crónica del desamor,

The paper in this book
meets the minimum requirements of
American National Standard for
Information Sciences—Permanence of
Paper for Printed Library Materials,
ANSI Z39.48–1984.

Library of Congress
Cataloging-in-Publication Data
Montero, Rosa.
[Crónica del desamor. English]
Absent love : a chronicle :
(Crónica del desamor) / by Rosa
Montero ; translated and with an
introduction by
Cristina de la Torre and Diana Glad.
p. cm.
— European Women Writers Series
Translation of: Crónica del desamor.
ISBN 0-8032-3141-5 (cloth)
ISBN 0-8032-8176-5 (pbk.)
I. Title. II. Series.
PQ6663.O55C713 1991
863'.64–dc20 90-28657
CIP

Publication of this book was assisted
by a grant from the
Program for Cultural Cooperation
Between Spain's Ministry of Culture
and United States Universities.

Contents

Acknowledgments

I am grateful to the National Endowment for the Humanities for the fellowship to the Literary Translation Institute, where the final revision of this translation took place; to my colleagues at the NEH seminar, particularly its codirector Gabriel Berns, for many helpful suggestions and constructive criticisms; and, most especially, to Erdmann Waniek for cheerful encouragement, incisive editorial comments, and terrific meals.

C.T.

A special debt of gratitude is owed to Dr. Johnnetta B. Cole, president of Spelman College, for her steadfast support of the value of literary translation as a scholarly endeavor.

D.G.

Introduction

In 1975, after almost forty years as dictator of Spain, Francisco Franco died. A country that for decades had been isolated from so-called corrupt foreign permissiveness regarding political, social, and, specifically, sexual mores was suddenly faced with the challenges of freedom. The subsequent shift from totalitarian rule to a constitutional monarchy required the delicate balancing of many opposing factions. It was carried out with a skill and determination that might well serve as a model for other countries attempting to dismantle the legacies of repressive regimes and build the basis for democracy.

Spain's transformation has been remarkable indeed, and not only for its swiftness in drafting a new constitution that guarantees civil liberties for all citizens. Tackling reforms on all fronts at once, the country has already made immense strides in catching up with the rest of Europe in other ways as well. For example, the economy has been diversified, the industrial infrastructure modernized, censorship lifted, labor unions and political parties legalized, church and state separated.

Furthermore, by freely electing a socialist government in 1982, thus bringing to power those vanquished in the Civil War, Spaniards appear to have closed that deeply divisive chapter of their recent history and to have passed a risky test of their newly established system of government. This atmosphere of excitement and innovation has been a boon to the arts. There has been a resurgence of creativity all across the spectrum, from architecture and design to painting, literature, and the performing arts.

Cultural evolution, however, understandably lagged behind. It was one thing to restructure economic and political institutions, and quite another to meddle with dearly held notions of how to live one's own private life, let alone to call into question the many written and unwritten privileges that men were accustomed to—to women's detriment—in a traditional society. For instance, men had full control of family finances, not only because they were usually the sole breadwinners but also because the law prevented even married women from having bank accounts in their own names before the new constitution was signed in 1978. Catholicism was the official national religion, and the Church wielded enormous power. As a result, marriages could be dissolved only by annulments, which were rarely granted; divorce did not exist, and thus remarriage was impossible; women had little recourse in case of desertion by the husband; abortion, under any circumstances, was a crime. Franco had subscribed to ultraconservative ideas about gender roles and had sought to enforce them through legislation and education. Two generations grew up under his repressive and paternalistic regime, and many Spaniards, both male and female, continued to think in conservative terms, particularly with respect to the position of women in society.

The words of an early Italian feminist, Sibila Aleramo, succinctly summarize the specific goals and obstacles in the fight for equality between the sexes. Written in 1907, in her seminal novel *A Woman*, they unfortunately still applied seven decades later to Spain:

> Feminism! Organizations of working women, protective legislation, legal emancipation, divorce, the vote in local and parliamentary elections. . . . All this will certainly be a massive task, but it will only scratch the surface: we have to change men's consciousness and create a new one for women![1]

As Aleramo well knew, this is much easier said than done. As Spanish women—indeed, women everywhere—found out, it is a long and difficult struggle.

The abolition of obsolete laws and the passage of liberal ones to give women a degree of control over their lives reflected not necessarily the general attitude of the people but rather the desire for change as pursued by a specific sector of the population.[2] Even though a sizable minority of urban men and women began to lead outwardly unconventional lives, just beneath the surface many still harbored traditional ideals that emerged in situations of conflict. As a consequence, women—and also men, to a much lesser extent—suffered from what has been called "split consciousness": the clash of old values with new aspirations, which resulted in a sometimes paralyzing anxiety. Men, even those who boasted of their liberal views, were reluctant to renounce the extraordinary power they had enjoyed all their lives and had come to consider their rightful claim. Women were often ill prepared, both emotionally and professionally, for some of the consequences of equality, such as going out into a world not overly eager to accommodate them. They soon realized that laws, though preventing some of the most blatant discriminatory practices, do little more than allow for the theoretical possibility of equality between the sexes. Lived equality goes well beyond legislation and affects every aspect of living, from something so symbolically charged as allowing a woman to become a cabinet member to scores of more complex territorial matters. Equality is a process internal to each individual as he or she relates to others and the world. It was quite clear that in the country that invented *machismo,* this would require a radical reassessment of cultural assumptions.

Thus the first decade (1975–85) following Franco's death, known as *la Transición*, was, not surprisingly, exhilarating but chaotic and disappointing as well. It was especially disturbing for young women, many

of whom had joined the student protest movement of the late 1960s to fight against a regime which basically believed that women should be neither seen nor heard. Having marched in demonstrations alongside men, having indeed risked their lives just as the men had, these women rightfully expected to be equal partners in the new society. It was not so. Changes in this realm followed a jagged path; efforts were often riddled with irony and achieved mixed results. In summary, both in the public and in the private sphere there was a gap between spirit and letter, word and deed, legislative goal and social reality. It was precisely the experience of this gap that made the matter of redefining the roles of men and women in society, as well as the relations between the two, so pressing.

Unavoidably, the first question that arises is who exactly should do the redefining? The new generation of women writers that emerged during the transition years took to this task.[3] Their aim was twofold: to elucidate the problems clearly and give women a voice in their possible solutions; and to articulate the nonexistent, or unheeded, feminine point of view and incorporate it into the contemporary experience, thus bringing some balance to the male-dominated public discourse. Rosa Montero, born in 1951, belongs to this group. In fact, she was named among the ten most influential women of the transition decade in a survey carried out by *El País*, Spain's most respected newspaper, for which Montero is a staff writer. She is an award-winning journalist and the author of five novels that have gained both popular and critical acclaim: *Crónica del desamor* (translated here as *Absent Love*), 1979; *La función delta* (*The Delta Function*), 1981; *Te trataré como a una reina* (I will treat you like a queen), 1983; *Amado amo* (Beloved boss), 1988; *Temblor* (Tremor), 1990. Rosa Montero's fiction is set in Madrid, a contemporary and recognizable urban environment;

her writings deal with basic human experiences: epiphanies and disappointments, discoveries and despair, commitments and betrayals. She writes at very close range of concrete daily incidents, the many small things that give life its flavor. Her writings are clearly focused on but not limited to recognitions; part of her appeal stems from revealing the obvious, which so often escapes us precisely because it is so evident.

Montero balks at the label "feminist author" because for many Spanish critics it is not a descriptive term but a dismissal. Furthermore, she denies that political activism is the motive for her writing. She may write *from* a specific camp but not *for* it. Her reasons for writing are strictly personal: to exorcise her private ghosts, to face the contradictions in her own life, and, in so doing, to arrive at an integrated self.[4] Nevertheless, her work fulfills one of the generally accepted goals of feminist writing: consciousness raising. She achieves it by voicing men's and women's intimate fears, exposing destructive patterns of behavior, confronting formerly private sufferings as public matters of social import. The fact that her first four novels have all been best sellers in Spain indicates that Montero touches a raw nerve and echoes the feelings of many of her peers.[5]

This first novel captures the atmosphere of the early years of *la Transición,* the birthing pains of the new consciousness. In it Montero explores the effects of social turmoil in the home and the workplace, in friendships and sexual encounters. What she finds is a tangle of unresolved tensions, conflicting interests, and ambivalence: the confusion of men and women forced to navigate the murky waters of radical change.

The linear narrative of *Absent Love* covers a year in the lives of a group of middle-class professional women struggling to find a place in the commotion and flux of post-Franco society. The novel begins at the point when the characters have realized that more is needed than "a room of one's own," when they have tried and failed, when love is over. Through the use of flashback and metafictional devices, Montero succeeds in enriching the simple story line with significant historical and personal details that cast it in a larger perspective. As the title suggests, the book tells the story of a lack, of the stinging absence of intimacy and grounding acutely felt by those who choose untraditional life-styles. Set against the specter of established traditional existence on the one hand and marginal subcultures of illusory value on the other, *Absent Love* emphasizes the undesirability of the available options and the desperate need for alternatives. But just how, exactly, to go about finding them? The feminist movement in the Spain of the late 1970s had not developed either an ideological base of its own or any kind of grassroots organization. Women were just beginning to articulate their needs and make decisions for themselves when freedom, and new possibilities for action and participation, came about. It was too much in some respects, not enough in others. Men, being in the position of power, welcomed the opportunity to shape the new society and tailored it to fit their desires. In other words, only the external conditions were altered, leaving intact the fundamental value structure of relations. Montero's characters reflect these sociological circumstances. They suffer from chronic disorientation, and most seem to flounder from one emotional false start to the next. Their basic goal is a negative one: they want to escape an obscure, resigned existence such as their mothers lived.

The characters' rejection of the submissive and limiting traditional feminine roles produces some positive results: they are all self-supporting women who find varying degrees of satisfaction in their careers. But relations at work are often problematic, since the stress of professional competition has been further complicated by the subtleties of sexual politics. After the initial excitement of independence has worn off, and with little to show except sagging skin and egos, the women begin to feel weary, adrift, afraid. Their youthful ideals have been replaced by loneliness, the central fact of their lives and the motif of the book. It is mostly the avoidance of loneliness that links the characters—loneliness in the present and the even greater threat of loneliness in old age, which begins to loom over these characters in their thirties and forties—that colors their actions and tinges them with urgency. Ana, the protagonist of *Absent Love*, is a prime example. She is thirty years old, a single working mother. Her attempts to find a network of support that will take the place of the natural family lead her into the company of other more or less displaced women and aging homosexuals who populate the fringes of society, self-exiled if not cast out from the mainstream. There is something both touching and pathetic about the desperate tone of these friendships, which are deepened by laughter and common calamities (such as no longer being prime candidates in the romantic market) but avoid the deceit or the power plays that mark professional and sexual encounters.

Montero weaves her story tautly between familiar binary opposites: masculine/feminine, youth/age, then/now. The emphasis of the book is on personal relations, particularly of the sexual kind, because the intimate realm is where the tension and confusion are manifest most crudely, felt most intensely. If before, women had been suffocated by the code of virginity that thwarted the development of their sexual nature, they were now victimized by a freedom that precluded the intimacy they sought. Sexual relations continued to be dominated by the immediate physical gratification that satisfies men, rather than providing for the more elusive and complex emotional needs of women.

Intimacy is the realm of vulnerability, and men—as fearful of failure, in Montero's portrayal, as women are of loneliness—prefer to reduce the risks, turning sex into a sport where success is measured by the number of orgasms. As a consequence, sex becomes a quantifiable and depersonalized endeavor; and the lovers, slaves to a performance rating. Establishing an open dialogue between men and women, one of the aims of feminism, proves to be equally difficult. New circumstances spawn new roles that preclude spontaneous exploration of different ways of communicating. The disjointed quality of those exchanges is expressed in the ongoing play between text and subtext: what is said versus what one would like to have said. Self-censorship is, after all, the first and only defense of the weak. Moreover, the ambiguous moans of the downstairs neighbors—their source, pleasure or pain, left unexplained—are symbolic of this chaotic situation and serve as the *leitmotif* of the novel. Initially, then, the longed-for freedom from sexual restraint does not bring about instant fulfillment; instead, it proves to be yet another burden for women.

It is to Montero's credit, however, that she struggles to remain impartial and acknowledges that women are not just victims but very active accomplices in this situation. Ironically, their first and basic betrayal is often of themselves. In fact, many admit to having confused liberation with the imitation of typically masculine attitudes. At times, women become their own worst enemies when, in their eagerness to be the equals of men, they reject everything labeled feminine and appropriate phallocentric idiomatic expressions demeaning to their own sex. Most of the characters in the book come to realize that they have fallen into this trap at one time or another. Indeed, the author stresses that all women are susceptible to it, particularly in times of personal or professional success.

The opening chapter presents the issues that are elaborated throughout the novel. In the first scene, which takes place at the newspaper for which Ana freelances, she is asked to bail out her male boss and do some after-hours busywork. She has no choice but to acquiesce because of her tenuous position in the ranks, even though it means another late night away from her young son. In spite of the fact that the setting is no longer the home, women are still in a traditional position: subservient to men. What little room there is for women's participation in Spain's new society seems to be at the bottom of it. Montero again keeps things in perspective by showing us the other side of the coin: the high price of success paid by men in terms of emotional castration, the result of years of manipulation for the sake of career advancement. The next scene replays the theme of subservience, this time in intimate relationships. Ana hastily rearranges her schedule to accommodate the last-minute invitation of a would-be lover. At work she at least balks at unfair demands, but in romantic relationships she falls back on the well-learned feminine arts of pleasing, reacting, agreeing, accepting. Once again, though this blatant contradiction, we are reminded of the difficulty of changing patterns of behavior acquired in childhood. If women are quick to compromise, it is not only because of their upbringing, or for the sake of their hopes for meaningful relationships—both at work and in their personal lives—but also because of their position of weakness. Without intimacy, life is reduced to the pursuit and exercise of power. And women simply do not have it.

Perhaps the most glaring absence in the book is that of a sympathetic heterosexual male figure, one who at least tries to have an honest and open relationship (interestingly, the one brief exception, Gonzalo, provokes only irritation in Ana). What the reader experiences, sharing the female point of view, is a parade of selfish, lying, manipulative men who want it all on their own terms. Nevertheless, in their imaginations, women endow these very men with the characteristics they seek in their efforts to find someone to love. The split consciousness that pervades the book is nowhere more sharply focused than in Ana's infatuation with her boss. He embodies all that she deplores, envies, and desires. He is powerful, arrogant, handsome. And married. Ana, who constantly begrudges her part-time status at work, deludes herself about the possibilities of a relationship that can be only part-time as well. Instead of accepting the limits of her reach, Ana allows herself the luxury of willful self-deception to avoid facing the truth, to continue in the pursuit of the elusive and empty ideal. Rosa Montero merges narrator and protagonist with a subtle shift of pronouns, which she uses often and skillfully, as she calls into question the very concept of romantic love:

> She is well aware that this love is pure make-believe. But so what? Are not all our loves—except perhaps the first one—simple castles in the air? It is possible that in light of daily dis-

> enchantments, I feel the need to invent a romance, to rediscover the sparkle of the schoolgirl crush on the teacher, to convince myself I'm still young, to spice up my tedious existence, to forget that I'm thirty years old and that life is escaping swiftly, banally, toward the death that we all carry inside. [chapter 4]

Ana repeatedly loses herself in this absurd pantomime of love, this dream of an encounter which she knows to be false from the start. At a critical juncture in her life she once again falls back on a familiar role: in this instance, Cinderella, who waits for the handsome prince to come to her rescue. It is clear, even though Ana never explicitly admits it to herself, that a liaison with the boss would solve both her personal and her professional woes. Her basic attitude represents a surrender: she expects salvation and validation to come from the outside, from the source of power and prestige, from the man. She still perceives the woman's main source of influence to be not in her intelligence, or her integrity, or her abilities but in her attraction as a female member of the species. Montero repeatedly traces the painstaking process of unlearning and relearning patterns of behavior—in many ways akin to mastering a new language—that must take place if women are ever to evolve out of the inferiority rut that is the result of centuries of marginal existence.

The novel ends with a small personal victory for Ana, a bitter victory drawn from deep disappointment. In spite of that, or because of it, it represents her decisive moment of self-affirmation, the moment when the inner and outer voices merge as she succeeds in stepping out of her subordinate feminine role. She is finally able to put into practice what she knows and believes: namely, that autonomy is a matter of standing up for oneself; that it is as simple, or as difficult, as speaking one's mind. By ultimately daring to say what she means, Ana seems to acknowledge her life with all its imperfections and to accept responsibility for her choices. Ostensibly, nothing has changed for her, but in fact, everything has changed because the way she looks at life and lives it is radically different. The beauty of her turningpoint is that it is not based on a fortuitous change of circumstances or on anything outside of herself.[6] The words of Josephine Humphreys, commenting on the nature of hope in today's society, are applicable to Ana's situation: "It is a hope more difficult than we are used to, a kind of faith ultimately stronger than any other, rising as it does from nothing, no promise, no sign, no miracle."[7]

Language is the expression of a person's innermost individuality; as such, it is primordial. A child begins to speak when the notion of separateness from the mother is established, and words become the link across the ever growing physical distance between them. Speech also signals a new stage in the development of personal or group identity. Language represents the most basic depository of culture, and it not only voices but, indeed, shapes the way the speakers think. Women's literature in general and Rosa Montero's work in particular show an acute awareness of language as a tool for personal and social transformation. Montero's works stay within the bounds of everyday language, capturing the magic of popular expressions that bring shared assumptions to the surface to be confronted and examined. If she occasionally resorts to clichés, it is not out of ineptitude or lack of imagination but in an attempt to illustrate how our lives are diminished when we ignore our own inner voice and naively accept expressions contaminated by society's ideology.

At the formal level, *Absent Love* achieves a balance of opposites: the chronicle is posed somewhere between what is considered a "male" genre, the novel, and the more spontaneous "female" literary form, the journal. Montero's use of metafictional techniques adds complexity to the narrative structure. Her self-reflective style, which constantly seems to question itself, allows for the inclusion of humor and irony.[8] On a purely thematic level, *Absent Love* is a story about growth and, as such, duplicates a pattern used in many novels by women, with some significant departures from it. It is notable not only for what it does, and does so well, but also for what it does not do. Montero is never content just to identify a scapegoat. She does not simply throw out accusations or wallow in self-pity, and she never gives in to the temptation of withdrawing into a private world, as is the case with such other Spanish feminist novels as Esther Tusquets's *Varada tras el último naufragio* (Stranded after the latest shipwreck, 1980) and Ana María Moix's *Julia* (1970). Instead, her characters, whatever their shortcomings, provide an example of involvement and determination. Through them, Montero examines the culture for the roots of the conflict at both personal and social levels; she exposes the damage that power plays do to relations of every kind; and she makes a case for honesty and individuality for men and women, both still trying to get out of their own gender-based straitjackets. Montero issues a strong warning against the lure of facile solutions (or the fairytale trap) with the final romantic fiasco, which mockingly subverts any false hopes women may still harbor of being rescued.

Absent Love succeeds, within its clear limits, in establishing links of public intimacy among the readers. Ultimately, it is tangible proof of the anticipated maturation of Ana, its metafictional author. These are the merits of the book. Its promise comes from imagining a future not only of equality but of cooperation and reciprocity between the sexes. This adds an implicit normative component to the novel and makes *Absent Love* a political statement, a form of feminist action aimed at achieving a common goal: a renewed consciousness freed from sexual stereotypes.

NOTES

1. Sibila Aleramo, *A Woman* (Berkeley: University of California Press, 1980), p. 154.

2. Franco's death coincided with another important event: the beginning of the

international decade of women, which can be credited with bringing feminist issues to the fore. *Crónica del desamor* was published in 1979, before the laws legalizing divorce and abortion (in such circumstances as rape, threat to the mother's health, and fetal deformity) were passed in the early 1980s.

3. Previously, a few women writers in Spain had achieved a degree of fame—such as Carmen Laforet and Ana María Matute—but they were isolated cases, and their writings were not suffused with a specifically female consciousness, to go back to Aleramo's words.

4. Interview with Cristina de la Torre, July 1985.

5. It is too soon to gauge the success and/or impact of *Temblor*, her most recent novel. However, it was a finalist in the Minerva Prize for European novels in 1990.

6. The absence of any religious feeling is noteworthy in a country that once boasted a population 98 percent Catholic. The Church lost much of its influence after it officially associated itself with the Franco regime. Participation in religious services is now minimal, particularly among the young, even though most Spaniards remain Catholic in name.

7. Josephine Humphreys, review of Jay Gunneman's *We Find Ourselves in Moontown*, *New York Times Book Review*, May 28, 1989, pp. 9–10.

8. For an excellent study of metafiction in recent Spanish literature, see Robert C. Spires, *Beyond the Metafictional Mode: Directions in the Modern Spanish Novel* (Lexington: University Press of Kentucky, 1984).

Absent Love

A Chronicle

One

"Listen, Ana, can you write the captions for these photos?"

"No way. It's ten already and Curro's waiting for me."

As usual on the night before the *Weekly News* goes to press, the newsroom is littered with rejected copy, crumpled photographs, cigarette butts, plastic cups caked with coffee. The vending machine in the hallway is empty—that contraption the management had installed in its never-ending search for efficiency, to save on those dead minutes, on those seconds lost from work in coffee runs by the staff. Whoever wants to pacify a stomach belching from nicotine has to go down to the second-floor offices of the *Daily News*, where an impressive array of vending machines offer plastic sandwiches, coffee-colored swill, sodas, and all the traditional junk food consumed by journalists. Such a display of automation is due to the fact that there are even more employees on the second floor, and they are always there, day in and day out.

"Oh, all right, let's see them. But as soon as I finish this I'm off, OK? I have to pick up my kid."

"Ah, the suffering mother's act with a twist: the single mom."

"Witty, very witty. Ha, ha."

From a glossy picture the leader of the conservative party stares back through crossed eyes. It is a particularly apt and malevolent shot.
2 "Fraga's sharp eyes . . ." No, no, that won't do—rrrrrr, the paper hisses as it is torn from the carriage. "Fraga: a serene look toward the future," that one is trite but what the hell can they expect at this hour. The next one, ahh, the next one . . . a smug Eduardo Soto Amón surrounded by photographers and VIPs. No explanation.

"What's this one?"

"Oh yeah, love, I forgot"—Mateo releases the word "love" as if he were calling a ceasefire, since it is 10:00 P.M., since he knows perfectly well that she does not have to write these captions, and since he is the type who prefers the soft-glove approach because a bit of diplomacy never hurts. "That's from a lecture on political economics that the boss gave at the Institute of Modern Studies, or whatever it's called, on Ferraz Street. I'll get you the details. No big deal, just scribble three lines about how well he babbled, and that's it. In any case, don't get carried away and make him look bad. As you know, Annie, bosses have very sensitive little hearts."

And Soto Amón's own little heart is ensconced as usual in an expensive silk shirt and a double-breasted suit, both so impeccable that they do not even seem pretentious. His blond hair is ever so carefully tousled and distinguished by a hint of gray. He is flashing his perpetually smart, wolfish smile. "Eduardo Soto Amón's lecture at the Institute of . . ."

"Daddy took me to the zoo, mommy."

"He is not your daddy, Curro, he is *my* dad and that makes him your grandfather."

"Oh, then my daddy is Tato."

"No, love, Tato is my brother. He's your uncle because he's also your grandfather's son."

"Ahhhh . . ."

Ana silently awaits further questions, waits for Curro to make up his mind. But the child keeps quiet and turns his attention to the buckle

of his tiny shoe. At age four he is learning diversionary tactics, perhaps already afraid to know. Does he remember Juan? Does he keep a smell, a shape, a shadow, any particle of that Juan whom he has not seen since he was five months old? The apartment is cold, and Curro has to be un- 3
dressed quickly, slipped into his wool pajamas, and put to bed. At least my mother has already fed him, I'm so tired. The apartment is cold and, worse yet, lonely. The walls are bare and the rooms almost empty. She turns on the radio, poaches a couple of eggs and absentmindedly nibbles on some toast, opens a Dashiel Hammett novel where she left off two days ago, tumbles into bed still dressed, and curls up in the blankets. The apartment is so cold and so alone.

They lived together three years. Three years or a little less. Three years too many, in any case. He claimed to be a writer, and he did in fact write frantically, just as frantically as he tore up whatever he had written. She fell for his outrageously shapeless sweaters, his long hair that brought out the sadness of his face, his extraordinary past, his uniqueness. Wrong. What charmed her was his passion and his words, they were like fireworks. He was clever, a juggler of language. He would create himself anew each day, each day a different fictional character. Maybe that was why he could not write.

"I've no idea why you put up with him so long, Ana, he was such a disgusting freeloader."

"He was not, don't be ridiculous."

"Well, what would you call him then . . . he lived off you for three years."

"Shit, Julia, you sound like a mother when you talk that way. There's nothing wrong with living off someone. When a woman lives off a man, as so many do, no one thinks of her as a freeloader, right?"

"Well, I don't agree with that either. But it's just that Juan was . . . OK, if you like I'll take back the freeloader part, but he was still disgusting."

Ana thinks it would be good to write something someday. Something about everyday life, of course. About her relationships with Juan, with Curro. About Pulga and Elena. About Ana María, who somehow missed the boat and who now is quietly consumed by the agony of knowing that she is old and inadequate. About Julita, one more broken doll after separating from her husband. About clammy hands, dirty dishes, personnel cutbacks, fake orgasms, phones that do not ring, patronizing colleagues, diaphragms, impostors, anguish. It would be *Ana's Book*, dedicated to each and every Ana, each so distinct and yet so alike. A book that would capture moments like this:

ANA: Hello?

VOICE ON THE TELEPHONE: Ana?

ANA: Yeah, speaking.

VOICE: Hi, it's Diego. How's it going?

Ana has either just come back from the dentist minus one molar, or she has menstrual cramps, or her mood has been warped by the long wait, by so many days hoping for a call.

ANA: Just great, and you?

DIEGO: Not too bad. Hey, are you busy tonight?

Ana has to put Curro to bed, or she has to finish a lengthy article that she has not quite figured out yet, or she has agreed to have dinner with a very dear friend who would be unreachable this late in the day.

ANA: No, I was just reading . . . why?

DIEGO: How 'bout dinner, then?

It takes Ana but a split second to decide to wake up early to write the article; she calculates how long it will take her to dress Curro and rush him to her mother's—who will no doubt resent having the kid back again; she thinks with suicidal melancholy about the friend she is about to stand up, rearranges the expression on her face to hide the sadness, wonders if she has any pills for her painful tooth or ovaries.

ANA: Sounds great. What time?

And she knows that she will go out and be charming, intelligent, compassionate, and witty, that she will play to the hilt the strong, independent woman role with neither demands nor tears, those detestable feminine faults. "You're a wonderful woman," he will say at some point during dinner with a detached note of admiration—as one compliments a good wine, a fine sonata, the delicate things that make life more pleasant—without putting into that phrase any more commitment than the breath it takes to utter it. And Ana will manage a quick, self-assured smile as she tries to swallow the shame of feeling ridiculous along with the aftertaste of her bleeding gums.

Or, perhaps, something like this:

JAIME: When do you have to get up tomorrow?

ANA: Hmmmm. How 'bout you?

Ana has learned to be cautious. She answers questions with other questions to diminish the risks of the battle. Jaime is an intellectual, a committed man who fears compromising words. Before and after making love they have brilliant, refined, neutral conversations.

JAIME: I have a meeting at eleven, so I'll have to get up an hour before.

Ana has to be at a citizens' lobby press conference at ten, or has promised to go with Elena to the doctor, or . . .

ANA: At ten? Yes, that works out for me too.

JAIME: Great, then we can have breakfast together.

Yes, they will have breakfast together, and there will be at least this fragile truce, even if in the morning things are studiedly hasty and cold, the goodbyes vague and uncomfortable with no allusion to their next date.

Or maybe this:

LUIS: You really have it made, you know . . . I have to go back to work now while you can stay at home with your music, doing nothing . . .

It is late afternoon, they have been together three hours. The oppressive summer heat slips through the windows and warps the roof of the old building—the disadvantages of living on the top floor. The room is broiling, and Ana's nude body glistens with the sweat of summer and of sex.

LUIS: I sure don't feel like leaving.

He is getting dressed and his sleek body disappears bit by bit, first the jeans, then the shirt button after button . . . Ana feels she loses him as he covers up his nakedness. They had not seen each other in a month, and finally Luis found a gap in his tight schedule. A gap that is always brief, always skimpy. Ana keeps her mechanical parting smile even after the door closes. The record ends, the ice cubes have melted, the dirty glasses on the table are reminders of a nonexistent party. Sprawled on a lounge chair incapable of movement, Ana lets the sweat drip down her sticky body. She has organized her day around these three hours, has skipped appointments, ignored deadlines. Now she is paralyzed by the uneasy stupor of his absence and at a loss for what to do. She feels ridiculous in her sweaty nakedness, alone in her steamy apartment, hopelessly free at this lost hour of the afternoon.

But writing a book like that, Ana dejectedly tells herself, would be banal, futile, endless, a diary of boring frustrations. She is slowly getting warm and begins to undress under the covers. The pants first, then the sweater. Not the socks yet, her feet are still frozen. She finally manages the cotton pajamas, panting from the effort and the contortions under her tent of blankets. In today's paper, which she leafs through before going to sleep, the bullet-ridden bodies of supposed Basque terrorists bleed, as do those of the boy caught in the crossfire that blew his brains out, and of the policeman and his girlfriend who were shot in their car while still sweaty from an evening at the disco, slumped across the steering wheel which sounded their death, death, death . . .

The phone rings. It is midnight and she startles. Ana races to answer it before the boy wakes up. It is a wrong number, a soft and monotonous voice asking for Marcos. "Is this 233-1121?" "Yes it is." The man verifies the number in the phone book with a noisy swishing of pages, admits his mistake, apologizes. "It's so late, perhaps I woke you" (and the cripple who was brutally beaten by the cops is in critical condition. It was in Guipúzcoa and the man was helpless on the ground, the wig that covered his shaved head slipped and exposed the still fresh scars,

the policeman hit again and again the pink, tender stitches). The man insists, with old-fashioned, unctuous politeness, on inviting her for a drink: you have such a sexy voice, you must be very beautiful (wild melee in the streets of Madrid as official tow trucks wage war on ille-
gally parked cars, insults, blows, some bloody faces and civic outcries), and it is absurd but Ana feels incapable of slamming the phone down on this man. "What's your name?" "Forget it." She knows herself weak and trapped in her own kindness, in her timid and exaggerated courtesy, and for those reasons she is now involved in this cheap telephone flirtation, the kind she thought was long extinct (a seventeen-year-old girl who had hitched a ride suddenly opened the door of a moving truck and threw herself out, the huge double tires crushed her, the driver must have been slow in reaching out his hand to catch her, the same hand that he had used to paw her), but finally, after a very refined repartee, Ana hangs up.

In the photo section there is a small shot that is almost lost between the opening of the new freeway and the group portraits of the fiestas in Jerez (the queen of the festivities, the daughter of landowners, is looking cross-eyed at the camera with a bouquet in her hands and an outlandish bun tottering on her head). There, in a corner of the page as if begging forgiveness, is the sad face of an insane man. "He does not know his own name," reads the caption. The man was taken to a hospital after being found wandering the streets like an orphan, having forgotten his identity, his home, his destiny. He is in his fifties, has a shock of unruly black hair, a flattened nose and pouting mouth, big innocent eyes, long-lashed eyes filled with fear. He is an ugly man, a decrepit and frightened man, and he displays his loneliness so clearly that it is threatening and burdensome, because it is immoral, indiscreet, and totally out of place to forget one's own identity.

The phone rings once more. "Hello pretty voice." It's that idiot again. He repeats his dated compliments and his spirited invitation. "Thank you, I don't drink," she says. "OK, then we'll have some juice."

He says he has just left the office: "I work for an architect, you know," he insists, convinced of his own importance, expecting that the mere mention of his profession will clear the way. "You surprise me," she says at last. "Why?" "Because I can't understand why you're pestering me, but I can think of three reasons: first, that you have nothing to do all day; second, that you are very lonely; and third, that you are very bored." The man all the while vigorously denies and complains. "And I, on the other hand," Ana continues, "have a lot to do, I am not alone, and I'm never bored. So don't call me again."

After hanging up, Ana feels high and proud of herself. She likes what she has said. It is odd how sometimes she is able to give appropriate and timely answers, and at other times she gets blocked, flat, and mute in tense moments. But this time she was great, she tells herself, even if she did lie a little about her loneliness. The man's, however, must be even greater, a wedded and shared loneliness perhaps, a subconscious loneliness as if he had lost himself—like the stranger in the photo—and did not know it yet, still believing his image of the architect's assistant and family man, unaware of its utter distortion.

RIIIIING!

"OK, that's enough!"

This time Ana has answered full of fury—that idiot is going to wake Curro up—and now hears a familiar voice on the other end.

"Hey, cool it. What's going on?"

It is Elena. Ana giggles, "Sorry, I thought it was the jerk who keeps calling to ask me out for a drink." "Wow, you sure lead an exciting life." "Well, we all have to make it through the night, you know."

"I've had a lousy day," says Elena still laughing. "All I need is for you to yell at me too."

"Why?"

"C'mon, it's not very pleasant to have someone pick up the phone screaming . . ."

"No, not that. Why'd you have a lousy day?"

"Oh, the usual . . . I had a fight with the head of the philosophy department and told him to kiss off, which means I'll be fired soon and, as if that weren't enough, Javier and I bickered all afternoon, for a change."

"Ahh, you guys are still at it . . ."

"I know, I know," Elena cuts in sharply, "but I don't want to talk about that now, I'm too angry. And besides, you know how hard it is to end a relationship . . ."

"What was it today?"

"I'm not even sure, something stupid, anything, it doesn't matter . . . let's just skip it."

"Fine. I'll see you tomorrow then."

"Yes, that's why I called, to remind you about the gynecologist. I have to work until five-thirty, so we better meet there."

"And your sister?"

"Candela will meet me after her classes. We'll go together."

Just as she is hanging up, Ana hollers, "Hey, wait," but the line is already dead, and all she hears is the exasperating dial tone. Naturally I can't remember the address. Well, it's all right, I'll look it up in the phone book.

She was almost ready, combing her hair absentmindedly and hastily in the bathroom, when she heard the voices again, the screams. Her brush stopped in midair; Ana remained paralyzed with fear for a few minutes, tensely facing her own image in the mirror, her ears straining to make out the noises. The meager light in the bathroom made the sobs piercing the floor, and her conscience, even sadder. This time it had started suddenly with a dry hoarse cry, only to break out after a brief pause into blows and the rasping sound of bodies or furniture being dragged across the floor and, worst of all, the pained helpless moans. She kept her ears peeled for a long time, but the concert organized by her neighbors gave no signs of winding down. Finally, she had to leave, run out of the apartment reverberating with noises and rush down the stairs. She was late and flew over the one hundred and twelve steps because the elevator is crafty and deceitful and refuses to take anyone down. Whenever a stubborn or foolish tenant risks the trip, he usually ends up stuck in the basement. So Ana is now out in the street, her ears still tortured by the screams. She is in the street, it is late, it is raining. Given her lack of an umbrella, the fact that the street is thick with sluggish traffic, that the bus is late as usual, that a cold and damp dusk is rapidly engulfing her, that darkness is approaching with insulting urgency—given all that, and with a feeling of surrender, Ana allows herself the extraordinary luxury of a taxi. This is going to cost a mint, it's absurd, if I had left earlier I could've saved this money, and it's such a tight month already.

"What number d'you say?"

"Thirty-seven."

The taxi driver turns his flat, pimply face toward her. He is a young kid with black curly hair, so thick that its weight seems to crush his face and crowd his features around his chin. He is decked out in dark leather, an outfit full of zippers, and spends the time humming and snapping his fingers to the hard rock that blares out of his tape deck. Funny how things have changed. Ana remembers when, not so long ago, she learned to be wary of taxi drivers. Be careful around them, she would tell herself; many are police informers ready to turn you in for anything remotely suspicious. Those were the Franco years, years filled with whispers. Now this kid drives with one hand, sings along to English rock lyrics, and his dashboard displays funny signs, handwritten with care in colorful ink: "Please don't mess with my head," and "Don't try to explain—I got it already." There are cassettes scattered on the front seat, in the glove compartment, on the back ledge, along with a string of red and green blinking lights that reveal his longing for the discotheque and make the car look like a speeding Christmas tree. At a stoplight the kid admits, "When my boom box doesn't work, I don't work," shouting at the top of his lungs because the music is loud, loud, loud.

The gynecologist is very trendy and has an office in a new development in the suburbs. The flashy highrise looms over shabby, aging little houses in the vicinity. Elena and Candela are already in the waiting room, you really are a drag, good thing we had to wait or else we would've gone in without you. It's Elena, in her quick and abrupt way, who snaps, while Candela smiles with ironic detachment. Candela must be close to thirty-five, and it shows in the puffiness around her eyes, in the corners of her thin, determined lips where fine wrinkles have begun to appear from all the teeth clenching required for survival, thinks Ana who feels a very special respect for her. The two sisters are remarkably different. Elena is slight, high-strung, and fiery. She is really striking, her amber cat eyes and thick, curly mane give her an exotic, burnished mulatta air. In contrast, Candela has large bones, a square jaw, an expressive almost tragic face, so pale and with such pronounced eyebrows that she could be a Greek actress, an Irene Pappas about to play Electra. Forceful. Candela is a forceful woman and everything about her (her way of sitting erect or resting her sharp chin in the crook of her thumb and forefinger) exudes an aura of wisdom and self-possession. She has a caustic, black sense of humor, developed perhaps as a form of defense. With wrenching irony she can reconstruct her baroque personal history (drunken ex-lover, domestic violence, economic woes, two kids, former mate who committed suicide, a whole life so packed with melodrama that it seems more fictitious than real) with such grace, with such convincing distance, that people actually laugh themselves to tears at the often told tale of how a certain young man threw himself out of a ninth-story window before her very eyes. Because of all that, Ana feels admiration, respect, awe for Candela's courage. And underneath it all, also a hint of fear.

"Hey Candela, how've you been?"

"Oh, I'm OK now, but it was a pretty close call."

Candela is convalescing, still ripped open as if from a Caesarean. It all began a while back when a Spanish gynecologist inserted an IUD. Doctor, I'm fed up with birth control pills and scared by the studies showing the high risk of stroke for women over thirty-five. I don't want to be a slave to that silly little pill month after month without even having a regular sex life. Doctor, I want to try a different method of contraception. After three months of wearing the copper wire, she got pregnant and went to London. There she had an abortion—a hygienic, a sterile, an international abortion. A bitter abortion, as usual, as always.

Ana thinks that if men gave birth, abortions would have been legal all over the world since the beginning of time. Which pope, what cardinal would dare deny a right that his own guts demanded? Politicians in their childbearing years would never overlook their own needs by asserting, as they do now, that abortion is merely one more method of birth control unscrupulously demanded by guilty women. And yet these guardians of genital law and order readily pay for foreign D & C's for their hapless daughters while other women have no recourse other than back-alley Spanish butchers. Women like Teresa, Juan's sister.

Ana had lived with Juan about two years when Teresa moved in. By that time their relationship was sheer hell. They had no money and had to share their dilapidated house with more and more people. First came the two Catalonians, then the photographer, finally Teresa. She was a strange woman, tough, and hard to get to know. When her unemployment check ran out, she started filling in as a hostess in an "American" bar. She did not have to sleep with the customers, of course not; she only had to put up with their drunken sob sessions and their wandering paws, eager to explore and fondle. In fact, Teresa took this job to help out her brother. Juan was talking about calling it quits and taking off for South America, putting behind him his anti-Franco militancy, his jail term, the beatings in prison dungeons, chucking everything and with it the image under which he gloried and suffered. When Ana met him, that Juan no longer existed—she later wondered whether he had ever been any different—and the thought of participating in anything remotely political terrified him. I'm too well known, I can't take any more risks. This was during Franco's last stage, a time of firing squads, death sentences, antiterrorist laws, when the country shivered in the cold sweat of fear. Ana, barely overcoming her own panic, would attend the demonstrations, her legs shaking, her jaw aching from clenching her teeth. When she returned home still flushed, her nerves raw, Juan would ask how things had gone and, without bothering to wait for an answer, would pass judgment: that rally was suicidal, you guys are fucking things up, the political situation clearly requires that . . . then, in the role of veteran militant has-been, he would proceed to spill out his theories.

The simple truth was that their relationship was crumbling and he needed some nonexistent funds to start again in the New World. Ana's job at the bank had paid the basic bills until her belly began to show and she was fired. That was when Teresa went to work at that joint—"just for a few months, it doesn't pay much but with the tips I'll make out fine"—and for weeks after, she saved for her younger brother, mothering him as usual, and always talking about how much she wanted to have a child. So, when one day she announced that she was pregnant, Ana asked if she planned to go through with it.

"No. No, I can't," Teresa replied somberly.

"But why not?"

"Because I can't, because I don't want it, because I've made a mistake, because I'm not even sure who the father is and anyway neither of them is more than a good friend, because we have no money, because your pregnancy is enough, because I want my child to be born under different circumstances. Because, just because."

She had almost fifty thousand pesetas stashed away in a chipped tin piggy bank—"It was the last present from my father, before his accident"—and Ana suggested that she use it to go to London, that's the only option, no way around it. But one night Teresa came back from work quite early, her eyes cloudy and swollen, and went straight to bed. "I didn't go to work today. Someone gave me an address, el Pozo del

Tío Raimundo. I went there this afternoon and they inserted a bamboo shoot, it will swell, stretch the cervix, and in a few hours I'll abort, I have to take some antibiotics and stay in bed, it only cost three thou-

sand pesetas." And Teresa kept to herself the search through unpaved streets for the rundown shack of the old midwife Doña Mercedes, the stench of cabbage and sewage, the low filthy ceiling blistered by dampness that she watched lying face up and legs spread while strange hands groped painfully inside her. On the dresser at her right there were some flowers in a plastic yogurt cup and on the wall a framed picture of Jesus. Teresa was stretched out on the dining room table and she could feel across her buttocks the heat of the bulb that lit the surgery. Three thousand pesetas.

When Ana returned home the next day, she found Juan holed up in the bedroom, irritated and gloomy. "Please Ana, go talk to Teresa, I'm sorry I can't deal with her, she's just unbearable." He was torn between guilt and fear. So she went to Teresa's room at the end of the hall, a dark, sad little room off the inner patio. Ana found her crying, bundled up in the covers. "What's wrong, are you in pain?" And yes, she hurt. She had taken the pain killers but she still felt as if there were a claw in her womb, but that was not the reason she was crying, it was because in the toilet she had seen the bloody shapeless mass fall out, my God, how awful. And Ana felt her own child suddenly heavy inside her. "Calm down, Teresa, you can have a child later on, whenever you want, but now you have to get well. Can I bring you some tea?" But Teresa went on sobbing inwardly, and Ana was frightened by those unseen tears. There was barely any light in the room even though it could not be past two. The air was thick and reeked of sweat, of menstrual blood, of tears. This is what poverty is all about, Ana thought as if in a dream, I'm living in abject poverty, it's exactly this, the pathetic daily filth without any hope of improvement. "Have you taken the antibiotics?" She touched Teresa's forehead; it was dry and burning.

She was awakened at dawn by an imploring voice, Ana, Ana. Teresa was holding on to the headboard for balance and clutching her belly, she was a shadow in the gray morning light. Ana, I'm very ill, please take me to the emergency room. She dressed quickly. Juan was sleeping soundly, or pretending to. Don't wake him, said Teresa, and Ana boiled with hatred for him. So they rushed out to the street in search of a taxi. There were very few at that hour, and it took a while to find one. Teresa sank shakily to the curb, her arms crossed over her belly, rocking herself back and forth. She was delirious with fever, her reality blurred, but she repeated obsessively, "Don't say a thing, Ana, they must not find out, we'll pretend it was a miscarriage." They took her straight to surgery, she must be dying, thought Ana with an aloofness that later shocked her. They sent Ana home—after all, they were not even related—she could visit the next day, room twelve, between two and four, if Teresa pulled through. And she did. All six beds in the ward were filled and the room overflowed with visitors, family members who tried to salvage some shred of privacy by whispering. Teresa was the only one all alone, her sheet pulled up high because they had not even thought of bringing a nightgown. She was ashen and exhausted. "You know, Ana," she said lowering her voice, "they were furious and asked what I'd done to myself, they suspect an abortion although the bamboo shoot fortunately doesn't leave the same marks as a D & C, the doctor told me that he'd been on the verge of not operating, that I was old enough to know what I was doing. They're bastards, Ana, really dangerous bastards." In the next bed there was an old gypsy woman, wrinkled and olive skinned; they had removed her uterus and she was moaning, "Oh lor', oh lor', oh lor' " with her family huddled around, a dozen people in bewildering chatter who paid little heed as she continued firing off her litany of complaints. When visiting hours were over, a doctor stopped Ana in the hallway. "Are you related to Teresa Zarza?" "No, I'm a friend." "Well, you two better watch out. I don't know why I don't turn you in this time, but if anything similar happens again, you're both going to jail." The man was tall with graying hair and he felt powerful in

They are now in the doctor's office and the smile on his boyish lips is condescending, disdainful. He is approaching middle age, has carefully groomed hair and baby skin. He sits very stiffly in his straight-back chair and rests his fingertips—in what he may well consider a dignified gesture—on the edge of the massive desk of heavily inlaid wood darkened over time, a desk probably inherited from his father, likewise a doctor, or from another relative, a lawyer perhaps. There he sits, observing them from afar with his round cow eyes, changing the inflection of his voice ever so slightly so that his well-considered disregard for the diaphragm can resonate.

"It's a poor method, I don't recommend it, it's risky, you'll end up pregnant."

"Well, it may not be the safest way, but I've already gotten pregnant with one IUD, and then I almost died from the infection another one caused, and besides, I don't want to stay on the pill because I've been on it for so long."

"But, my dear"—and the man waves his hand emphatically, sweeping away Candela's objections—"the diaphragm is a disaster waiting to happen, in a few months you'll be back with yet another swollen belly . . . and besides, it's so messy, so . . ."

"I've been using it for four years," Elena pipes in, "and it has worked for me."

"Oh really?" answers the doctor skeptically. "Then you've been lucky. And how do you do it? Do you cut the guy off and put him on hold?"

(There is a characteristic shared by many gynecologists: their disdain for the individual, the sheer rudeness of these great macho cunt inspectors.)

"What's that?"

Elena has taken the diaphragm from her purse, a small round plastic container that looks like a toy compact powder case. The man opens it without much interest and the powder that coats the rubber spills across his desk, sinks into the inlays, and leaves a fine mist that generously covers his medical trousers. He reddens, his voice screeches effeminately, "What is this?" He is enraged and holds the white disc between two timid fingers.

"Talcum powder so that it won't crack."

It is clear that this is the first time the doctor has seen a diaphragm. It is clear that he finds it disgusting, that it perhaps reminds him—as it does many men—of the hated condom. The pill, the IUD are the woman's problem. She is the one who uses them and suffers the consequences. The diaphragm, however, affects the couple: Must the male interrupt his warm-up exercises so that she can insert the rubber disc? Preposterous. Must one also use a spermicidal cream? Disastrous. Especially when the pill and the IUD are so convenient and the man need not bother . . .

He charged them one thousand pesetas apiece. "What a waste, that idiot had no clue what a diaphragm was, what a crock," raves Elena biting the air. "I'm not claiming that it's the ideal method, that just doesn't exist, but at least it doesn't do too much physical harm, and it ticks me off that no male gynecologist will even acknowledge its existence." They walk quickly to the car, chilled to the bone by the wind. Ana laughs, "It's remarkable that women all over the world are returning to the relative safety of the ancient diaphragm." Candela agrees, "That's right, I know mother used it, she had it brought from France, she told me that the outer ring used to be hinged and at times would pinch." "That's awful," winces Ana. "How primitive," Elena chimes in and adds, "Mom used it?" "Yeah, that's what she told me." "It's odd," says Elena doubtfully, "she never mentioned a thing to me." "Maybe you never bothered to ask." By now they are back at their little car. "Shit," Elena hollers, "they've swiped my cassettes." The right window vent has been forced open. "Damn it, this is the second time already, this little trip to the gynecologist has sure been profitable." "At least," Candela points out, "we have the consolation of knowing that the doctor is going to be brushing powder off his desk for quite a while." Laughter. "Can you still see the expression on that jerk's face?" As they start up the car in the gathering darkness, Ana notices a very thin woman of indefinite age, with vacant eyes and a drooping lower jaw, a mere wisp dressed in shocking red and propelled along the empty sidewalk as if by the wind, flapping her arms wildly, laughing and mumbling crazed phrases over her bony shoulders into the void. A pathetic woman, all alone, who passes them sticking out a pointed tongue, a moist and purple tongue that is somehow obscene.

Ana has just realized that there is nothing even remotely edible at home. So, to fool and appease her growling stomach, she makes a cup of herbal tea with an ear fixed on the breathing sounds of her sleeping son. As she slips into bed, cup in hand, Ana anxiously reflects about her days that seem to vanish, to be nonexistent. There are weeks, shadowy cursed weeks, burnt up in abject boredom from which only the comforting thought of her bed remains, as if the days had been rubbed out, transformed into a succession of dreamless nights. She sips her tea and thinks about Candela's scarred belly, the absurd powder on the desk, that woman's bared tongue that was just as shocking as the genitals of an exhibitionist. She shivers as much from sadness as from cold and turns out the light, eager to sleep. She feels restless, stressed out over something undefinable. She tosses and turns in her bed, her legs tucked up, hoping her feet will get warm. She is edgy and, for a moment, considers masturbating but quickly discards the idea. Today she is not up to even the slightest effort of fantasy necessary to pull it off. What she really craves is the sensual tenderness of sleeping entwined with a man, feeling his kiss on her shoulder. Self-knowledge comes so hard . . . when she broke up with Juan, she lost all trust in commitment. Ana thought her disenchantment was permanent and gloried in the first few months of rediscovery and reappropriation of her own space. The bed was again hers, her time was her own, there were hours when she was accountable to no one. Her individuality, her friends, her tastes, her decisions, everything that for three years had been shared was once more hers and hers alone. For months she could not bear the idea of sharing her bed, and those were months of plenitude, golden moments when she felt self-sufficient and free, when she began her career in journalism and knew her own strength, when she kept her emotional distance in relationships, much as a man typically does. But it has been four years now since that parting, and the old longings are stirring anew. Past experience makes her dread the very notion of living with a man, which she considers inevitably destructive, but she is tempted once again to exhaust the possibilities, to get to know a man in all his dimensions, to give the couple one more shot even though she fears it may be suicidal. And so, more than for sex, Ana yearns for the awkwardly sweet embrace of a sleeping lover.

Juan. When she left him it was for good. She could not bear to see him anymore, she simply could not. Now, however, Ana regrets it for Curro's sake. The boy needs a father's presence; he needs to stop being different from other kids. "Let Curro lead the way, don't mention his father unless he asks, then just answer his questions." This is Candela's advice, so it must be sound. She knows a lot about such things, and not only because she is a child psychologist but because she has had two children out of wedlock. Still, Ana wonders if it would not be a good idea to get in touch with Juan, to write to him in Colombia:

"Juan, I guess this letter comes as a surprise. Don't worry, I'm not going to get dramatic or, much less, nostalgic. I'm not going to dwell on past resentments. I'm writing because of Curro. He is four years old, and regardless of our mistakes and bitterness . . ." No, no. She recalls the letter she started two nights ago and blushes with shame. How corny—the relationship with Juan was so melodramatic that everything to do with him turns into a cheap soap opera.

Might as well face it, she is definitely not sleepy tonight in spite of the fact that she very much wants to be rested tomorrow for the heavy day ahead. At one o'clock she has an appointment with Domingo

Gutiérrez, the editor of the magazine. She is going to ask for, or rather demand, a permanent job. She has freelanced there long enough, and her position is still up in the air; she is a nonperson in administrative terms, lost in the monstrous bureaucracy of the *Weekly News*. Since
she hardly knows Domingo, Ana rehearses mentally what she will say, knowing all along that as soon as I sit down in front of the guy my mind will go blank even though I know I'm right. It could be this stress about tomorrow that is keeping her awake and, as in other involuntary vigils, Ana begins to hear strange noises in the apartment; the air is charged with danger, and her room reverberates with echoes and fills with sinister shadows. Ana feels her neck stiffen, her muscles tighten, the fear take over. But with practiced effort she controls it, laughs nervously at herself and tries to relax. One must not panic, the boogeyman must be kept at bay. Otherwise she might end up like Pulga, who tiptoes every night through her dark and lonely apartment in childlike terror, groping along the walls and expecting to find around each and every corner the shadow of the stranger of her most hidden fears. And so, gritting her teeth against the noises of loneliness, Ana finally falls asleep.

Two

"Good God. Here comes Ramses to oversee the work of his slaves . . ."

Ana rarely, or often but rather fleetingly, catches a glimpse of Ramses–Soto Amón, the brilliant and triumphant overlord of the empire of words, of the kingdom of the *News*. Soto Amón who owns two magazines and a newspaper, a publishing house, a distributorship, a press agency, and two literary awards is now scheming to take over a television network by snatching it from the claws of his fellow predators. Lately too, there was his appointment as member of the new Parliament. (Eduardo Soto Amón is a keen politician who has climbed unpredictable paths to power by hiding his political ambitions behind an elegant disdain for elected office.) A young senator of forty-two, he has the well-preserved look of the modern exec—the face of an intellectual, the steel-blue voracious eyes of an eagle, and the body of a jock. He is the ideal playboy on the cutting edge, practicing politics on weekends while keeping in shape with tennis or rowing. Sophisticated and powerful, the very epitome of the ruling class, he basks in the splendor of his achievements. He is the type that Ana has always loathed.

“Your boss is something else,” her friends would say.

“Who? Ramses?” Ana would answer with well-disguised anxiety.

“Ramses! Is that what you call Soto Amón? Ramses!”

“Sure, he’s the pharaoh of this great house of words.”

“Wow, that really cracks me up. He never did pay me and Jean Paul for a cover design he had us do. He’s a gangster, a real sonofabitch.”

Ana would always agree, with the tight-lipped smile of an accomplice in crime.

Mateo says that Ramses is coming today to oversee the work of the slaves, but he knows all too well it is not true. In fact, the all-powerful Soto Amón usually does not show much interest in the countless employees of his corporation. He holes up in his plush executive suite, receiving politicians or leaders or bankers, plotting clever scenarios and conspiracies. He never bothers with the strictly journalistic side of the business, and the more wicked tongues claim that is a blessing, since he knows nothing about it. He has, however, been sharp enough to surround himself with a highly capable staff and, with rare ability, has instilled a spirit of dedication and service by bullying them with his presence and tyrannizing them with his aloofness. He is the kind of man who knows how to endear himself by inspiring hatred and inflicting pain.

Mateo knows it better than anyone because he has been around the longest. He began to work for Soto Amón when the company published a small business weekly, *Basics*, that folded long ago. Fifteen years of collaboration, Mateo recalls, fifteen years. They were both quite young then and, after meeting their demanding weekly deadlines, would go on all-night binges. These would turn emotional as Eduardo, through alcohol-laced fumes, bared his anguish over the price he had to pay to keep afloat. Those were the nights when they loved one another more than they had ever loved any woman. Then Mateo was his closest ally, the one who fulfilled Ramses’s need for a faithful assistant, the one who could share his responsibilities and his sorrows. It was later that things got complicated as the years and successes accumulated. Now Mateo is editor-in-chief of the lead magazine, and he hardly ever sees Ramses. Now Eduardo Soto Amón does not even know the people who work for him. The newspaper staff swears that he has never set foot on the

second floor. He does stop by on the third, though everybody knows it is only to talk to Domingo about the *Weekly News*. The fact is that now Domingo Gutiérrez is his right-hand man, the heir apparent, his confidant and friend, whom Ramses is grooming to be the director of the leading newspaper and eventually to succeed him.

Domingo is lean and thirtyish and has a brilliant academic record heavily endowed with honors and Harvard degrees. He is a shining example of the new wave of journalists who speak three languages fluently. The training these young people get is really marvelous, as Soto Amón would say. Mateo thinks that his place in the inner sanctum has been usurped by the young Domingo because of his British accent, because . . . well, why not, because he is the new kid on the block. The director of the magazine knows only the brilliant, successful Soto Amón; disillusioned Mateo has seen him when he was down, when he made mistakes, when he could not make up his mind. Mateo simply knows him too well and that makes Soto Amón uncomfortable. Bearing a grudge like a jilted lover, Mateo indulges in snide remarks about Domingo: "Such a nice boy, isn't he? Have you noticed how he's acting more and more like Soto Amón every day? Peculiar, huh?" And it is true that Domingo has taken to crossing the newsroom with his hands clasped behind his back like the great Eduardo, with the same air of being above it all. What the director of the magazine perhaps does not realize is that Soto Amón's coldness has been honed over dark and difficult years of struggle for survival. Domingo, on the other hand, is fresh from the protective folds of his moderately liberal family and behaves like a college buddy, like another fraternity brother. He comes across as altogether too soft, too meek and confused, to take control of such an inhuman empire any time soon. He is a half-baked heir. But Mateo has said, "Here comes Ramses to oversee the work of the slaves," and sure enough, today Soto Amón has shown up, aloof and impeccable, cutting through the air of the main office with his sharp profile.

Ana recalls the day she turned thirty, that bitter day when she said goodbye to her twenties, to her youth, to her belief in a wide-open future. That was the day when she saw him make his appearance at the office, so self-satisfied in his gray suit, arranging his tie either out of habit or perhaps simply to caress the soft silk with smug approval. Eduardo was talking with Domingo, and Ana could overhear his voice, serious and measured with a hint of affectation: "Olivares told me so, and you know what an asinine fool he is." "So how did you deal with him?" Domingo's smile was already twitching at the corner of his lips. "I thanked him profusely, patted him on the back, and booted him out the door." Just at that moment, the graphic artist joined the two of them and whispered into Soto Amón's ear. That was when the unthinkable happened.

"Yes, of course, Andrés, of course," Eduardo stammered. "Sorry, man, but it completely slipped my mind. With all the pressure mounting up, well . . . forgive me, I'll sign that order today."

And, yes, Ana thought she saw him blush. The untouchable minor god of destinies—with so many workers in mortal fear of his very presence—blushes! So he was capable of emotion after all, the steely Eduardo. Perhaps he was shy, maybe even human, beneath his perfectly packaged image. And it was right then and there, disarmed by the surprising tint of his cheeks, that Ana was shocked to realize that she had a crush on Soto Amón.

Today, while she nervously spies on him from afar, pretending to pore over some papers, Ana feels that sharp longing, that almost physical pang of emptiness you experience when you think you're in love. It has been a month since her amazing discovery, and Ana still trembles whenever Soto Amón—so detached, so metallic—struts in. There, at the back of the room and totally unaware of her, the mighty Ramses smiles, poses, spins on his heels, and finally disappears out the door, painfully off limits. "Neighbors—be at the demonstration on the twelfth." Ana has to reread the pamphlet she is holding in order to make any sense of it. It is an appeal from the Coordinator of Neighborhood

Associations to attend a demonstration against housing speculation, tonight at eight o'clock. Ana sighs. Gone are the years of uncertainty and dread, years of rushing in panic from illegal demonstrations against Franco when she had forced herself to show up, her legs trembling with fear. Later came the death of the dictator, the so-called democracy, the apathy. Ana thinks that the public disenchantment, so often mentioned lately, is an invention of the new government, the Christian Democratic party: it is much easier to manage a country of cynics than one of fervent activists. Nevertheless, while trying to fight the paralyzing inertia, she too is perplexed by the absurdity of it all. Ana agrees with Elena's assessment, of course Ana agrees. The political parties are defunct, and new approaches are needed. The time is ripe for feminist caucuses, grassroots organizations, and common causes. Nevertheless, Ana will not be going to tonight's demonstration, nor will she attend the general rally that she knows to be absolutely right and necessary. Crushed by a skepticism that sinks her into inaction, she betrays herself by indulging a make-believe love for Soto Amón, in an individual and solitary escape from the real issues.

But it is time for her appointment with Domingo. Good luck, cutie, says Mateo; it will be a few minutes, says the secretary. Ana sits down on the leather couch in the reception room, stares at the paintings on the walls, and mentally rehearses her speech. She remembers that she has to buy Curro a pair of boots on sale. Nervous and crestfallen, she bites her nails, paces the floor, checks the clock, says to the secretary, "He's taking his sweet time," and answers her commiserating smile with a grimace. She sits down again, it's almost two o'clock. Finally the door opens and Soto Amón struts out with his quick pace, looking straight ahead and saying nothing.

"I'm sorry to have kept you waiting, Ana," apologizes Domingo, who is basically a polite man without too much imagination. Since he is short, the huge modern desk overpowers him as if he had inherited it from an older and bulkier brother. "Go ahead," he adds, lighting a cigarette. Ana begins, "Well, look, I've been working here for quite a while, and I still just fill in, even though I do the work of an editor, you can ask Mateo." "Yes, he's spoken well of you," says Domingo, and she insists, "No one would put up with this, I'm ready to quit." "Don't be so impatient." "It has nothing to do with impatience; I have a son to support and I need job security." "I'll see what I can do, you know it's not up to me," says Domingo. "I suppose it depends on Soto Amón, like everything else"—Ana immediately regrets her words—"Hey, not like everything else," Domingo takes offense, and Ana loses control, "Well, anyway, you and Soto Amón are such pals, so . . ." Domingo looks suspicious. "Why do you say that?" Ana realizes that she is botching things up. "Because it's common knowledge, everyone says you're his successor . . ." (What a jerk I am, she thinks, nervously scratching at the arm of the chair.) Domingo turns beet red and replies, "I'm successor to nobody," and there follows an embarrassed silence. He finally regains his composure and once again manages an affable smile. "What you ask seems fair enough, but you know we won't be adding any full-time positions until the end of the year." "But this is January!" Ana wails, and Domingo insists, "In any case, the rules clearly state that there will be no permanent openings until December. In a firm as large as this, we have to adhere to a system or else it would be pure chaos." And the next thing she knows, Ana is standing in the hallway. Booted out the door, as Soto Amón would say.

Three

Just as she was turning the key in the lock, Elena realized that she had forgotten to buy milk for breakfast. There's no way that Javier might have remembered. No, of course not. But as soon as she opened the door, she ran to the kitchen anyway, only to find the refrigerator empty as usual, and now where in the hell am I gonna find milk at this hour.

Elena thought for a split second—she really hates to wake up and have to face the day without breakfast—and raced back to the street. It was ten-fifteen and there was nothing she could do but get back into the car and drive to one of those awful all-night drugstores. Tonight Elena is thoroughly worn out and depressed after having spent a drenched afternoon at a poorly attended demonstration; it's really pathetic when only five thousand people show up. The fact is, she hadn't felt like going either; it had been drizzling and her mood was about as gloomy as the sky. But something still remained of her old activist habits, five years of group discipline had ingrained in her a willingness to volunteer and a yearning for action. So she went. In spite of everything, the rally had its nice moments. Entire families showed up, tottering grandfathers and nursing babies. But also some guys from union headquarters, who forced their way to the front with their pickets and banners—"Down with rent speculation!" "Decent housing at decent prices!"—followed in huge letters by the initials of their respective unions. It was the usual attempt to capitalize on what had started out as a nonpartisan effort. Elena was hoarse from arguing with them, "Back off, no banners are allowed up front," but they unflinchingly pushed ahead to the front ranks, where they allowed their pictures to be taken as eagerly as movie stars. Tomorrow the news of the march would be in all the papers, and the initials of those damn labor unions would appear, again, in all the photos.

Elena is upset about it and annoyed with her own behavior as well. She knows she has an aggressive streak and is afraid that she will lose control under stress and turn into that most unpleasant of characters: a woman on the verge of hysteria who spits out her words while frothing at the mouth, choking on her own rage. This afternoon she had insulted a tough-looking old man. "You, get back with that picket," she had bellowed. And the man, his face inscrutable, had looked straight through her and paid no attention. Otherwise, the demonstration went off without a hitch . . . except for the two neofascists that showed up. They were just kids barely out of their teens who, from the center of the crowd, flashed the Nazi salute and started hurling insults. What idiots, they almost got beat up. If it hadn't been for a group of union members who yanked them away, they would have been lynched for sheer stupidity.

Danger. Elena can still remember those years that seem so long ago, her first years studying at the University of Madrid: Spanish, Arabic, Latin, daily attacks by the mounted police, horses spewing smoke from their nostrils, philosophy, art history, geography, protests, sit-ins, buses set afire—Elena had known fear. When she was kicked around that day at Café Zulia (she was down on her hands and knees in shrimp peels and broken glass; the rioters had crashed through the door, followed by an onslaught of clubs, helmets, panic, and screams), she made the decision to join the Communist party to find out why she ran from the riot police, to counteract her fear with an awareness of the struggle. It was just around the time when all civil rights were suspended.

A lot of things were happening then. She left home for good and moved in with her sister. (She had turned nineteen, and it was not all that difficult; Candela had already blazed the trail, and Elena had never been that close to her parents.) That was when she made the dual decision to major in philosophy and to shed her virginity. One cold and damp winter afternoon, Elena walked into Café Tobi shaking the December rain from her hair.

"What a crummy day . . ."

It is almost Christmas, and the cheap bar is decorated with a scrawny tree pathetically strewn with tarnished tinsel.

"Hey, I've got an idea. Why don't we go to my folks' cabin in the mountains? I've got the keys, and we could build a fire and all that . . ."

Elena feels her stomach knot up with anticipation and dread. Today is the day. She has seen Miguel Angel around the university, but it has only been in the last week that they have ever really talked, that she has started to like him. She could not stand him before, the first-born son of wealthy parents, so luxuriously blond, so proud of his looks, so convinced of his charm. Then one day they talked for quite a while. (What was the reason—some class notes, a mutual friend?) They got along, they laughed a lot. That evening they saw a movie, the next day they had drinks and swapped kisses, one night later they were dancing and petting furiously with the unabashed enthusiasm of youth. In spite of his candid sophistication, Miguel Angel is merely two years older than she. They are both young, attractive, full of life, and Elena is smug with desire. She tells herself that Miguel Angel has appeared at the opportune moment. She had been such a prude—sweet sixteen and never been kissed and had not liked it when she finally was. Like so many other girls, she was reared in ignorance and contempt of sex. Yes, it has been a long road, but today she feels ready to lose her virginity.

She has gotten in touch with her body and has allowed herself to accept her own sexuality. And she knows that this afternoon she will go all the way in a not too distant mountain cabin.

"Great, let's do it."

Miguel Angel drives into the dark; it is barely five o'clock, but the low clouds have severed the daylight. He is in a good mood—or perhaps nervous—and chats freely, cracks jokes, delights in his own cleverness. Elena just sits there with that placid expression, somewhere between cheery and bovine, which she catches in herself whenever she thinks she is in love. Deep down she is a little afraid, won't it hurt? . . . the painful tearing of the hymen, the guilty blood stains on her thighs and sheets, she recalls the old wives' tales from her childhood. Bah! Nonsense. Elena feels splendidly ripe to take the step. She is not even worried about getting involved. Miguel Angel may be the first, but she is sure he will not be the last.

"Well, we're here. It's that one on the end."

The cabin has all the trappings of the typical family weekend retreat—inexpensive practical furnishings, a few decorative items of dubious craftsmanship, the sort of bric-a-brac that you certainly would not want in the Madrid house—and upstairs at the end of the hall many identical bedrooms, so impersonal that it could pass for a hotel. "The place is freezing," says Miguel Angel, "let's start a fire." He returns with an armload of logs and, in a flash, both are stretched out on a rug in front of the fireplace, playfully sharing a snifter of cognac.

"Shall we go upstairs?"

They have been hugging, kissing, rolling on the floor. Elena is slightly breathless, and her face is flushed from the flames of the fire logs.

"Yes, let's . . . but I must warn you I'm a virgin, and I'm not on the pill."

Miguel Angel pulls away and props up on his elbow. "You, a virgin?" He has gotten serious all of a sudden, and there is distrust in his voice.

"Yes. I mean it."

He hesitates, tries out several possibilities—smiles, frowns, gapes, blinks—but cannot decide which pose to take. He is completely thrown off guard. "That's impossible," he finally blurts out. "What kinda game is this?" Elena is dumfounded by such a reaction and gets the dreadful feeling that something has gone wrong. But no, it can't be, that's absurd.

"Don't be silly, Miguel Angel, why should I play games? Yes, I'm a virgin, and I tell you I'm almost ashamed to admit it. I just don't think that this virginity stuff is worth the fuss. I want to make love to you, and I wanted to warn you, that's all."

Miguel Angel stares straight through her. Elena leans toward him, "Hey, c'mon, what's the matter?" She makes her voice sound cheerful and kisses him lightly on the lips. It can't be that the spell—the fire, the laughter, the caresses—is broken, and for such a petty reason.

They go upstairs, cognac in hand, without exchanging a word. Elena is intimidated and smiles into the silence. In the master bedroom, the only one with a double bed, they somberly get undressed. It is the first time that Elena has seen a naked man and, in that tense atmosphere, feels ill at ease. She carefully avoids staring at his penis. "Let's get into bed, it's freezing," says Miguel Angel. Buried in the sheets, they stare at one another from across the bed. Soon he hugs her, begins to kiss her. She notices that his movements are clumsy; something is not working, and in her inexperience she blames herself. They press against one another in frustration, she does not dare touch him, and the air between them is turning icy. Finally Miguel Angel pulls away, "I don't want to make love to you." "But why?" she asks, ashamed of being a virgin, feeling rejected and humiliated.

"Because if you're a virgin, you'd better find someone who deserves you."

"What do you mean, deserves me? But . . . but that's ridiculous! What're you talking about? It's you I want, I don't get it."

"I don't deserve you, I simply don't deserve you."

"Will you listen to me?" Elena tries to make sense out of this madness. "You're more hung up on virginity than I am, for me it's just a fact, what are you afraid of?"

Elena is at a loss for words. Stunned, she tries to brush away the cloud of shame that blocks her thinking—can there be something I don't know, something I'm totally unaware of? Can this be a normal reaction? She feels so confused, so totally ignorant of sex. Finally, she leans forward to run her fingers through his hair. He remains tense and remote.

"You're afraid that since I'm a virgin, I'll never let go of you, that you won't know what to do with me. Is that it?" she ventures, trying to make light of it. Miguel Angel says nothing and stares at her from the safety of the blankets he has hastily pulled up.

"Hey, don't be silly. It's not my fault I'm a virgin, we're born that way, you know. There's a first time for everything, this is just a coincidence, c'mon, I have no intention of trapping you."

He does not seem to hear her as he retreats to the edge of the bed, mumbling, "I'm not worthy, I'm not worthy," and observing her distrustfully. At last, after minutes of silence, he checks the watch that he had left on the nightstand. "We better go." They get up and start to dress. Elena stifles the urge to cry. They go down to the living room and stamp out the fire. The night has closed in, and it is so cold outside that Elena thinks the sounds would not pass through the frozen air even if she could utter a word. They drive in silence for a few kilometers along an empty and endless stretch of road. Elena feels catatonic, incapable of making a movement or a sound. Suddenly Miguel Angel turns into a dark frost-scorched field and stops the car.

"What're you doing?"

Without replying he turns toward her, lightly caresses her hair, and plants a quick kiss on her cheek. Now Elena really is about to burst into tears. She had felt so lonely and rejected without knowing why—and not knowing made everything more painful—and that kiss set things right again. Everything's OK, now we'll figure a way out of this nonsense. She longs to press against his shoulder, to feel loved and caressed, but Miguel Angel gently stops her.

"Please . . ." his tone is imploring, breathless. "Please, caress me."

He opens his fly, he is hard, erect. It is the first time Elena has dared to look at the sex of a man.

"Touch me, please, touch me . . ."

Elena does not know what to do; she is flooded with anguish. He takes hold of her hand, slowly guides it to his penis, and clasps her palm around his tight warm flesh. She is not in the least bit excited; she feels empty, abandoned, unable to respond. She touches him ineptly, with some reluctance and disgust.

"Suck me," he says slowly, in a murmur. "Suck me," he insists.

Elena hesitates, she is repelled. Miguel Angel gently but firmly pushes her head down; at first she resists but finally gives in. She feels so clumsy, so guilty for not knowing how, she hopes that Miguel Angel once again will show some affection and barely understands what he expects of her. She opens her mouth and sucks him, his sex is hot and tastes salty, she tries not to think of it. From between his legs she sees the brake and gas pedals surrealistically illuminated by the dim overhead light. She concentrates on those shapes and makes her mind go blank until, suddenly, she feels something hot and slimy burning her throat. She is aghast: in her naiveté it had never occurred to her that he would ejaculate, but that is just what he did, he came in her mouth. Racked by nausea, she bolts and lowers the steamed-up window. The cold hits her in the face and creeps down her neck. Elena spits furiously onto the ground, again and again. She scrubs her mouth and her tongue with the back of her hand. He looks at her as if from afar, mumbles an almost inaudible "sorry," pulls out a handkerchief, wipes himself off, and starts the engine.

It has begun to snow and the flakes give an eerie dimension to the strip of night framed by the car lights stretching out before them. They say nothing for forty kilometers, but this silence does not bother her. Elena does not try to speak, nor does she feel like crying; she is aware only of her revulsion and anger, of her need to get home as soon as possible, to get out of his car and never see him again. They slowly approach Madrid, and while watching the whirling dervish of falling snow, Elena thinks about her upbringing, about all those mothers, aunts, and grandmothers who taught her that man was a vile creature whose only thought was to get into bed with you. If they only knew how tough it was to get one, as they say, to deflower you . . . The mere thought is so ludicrous that she bursts into peals of laughter, into wild inexplicable shrieks that Miguel Angel notes out of the corner of his eye in horrified silence.

(Elena was so traumatized by that experience that for years she could not bring herself to kiss a man's penis. Not until she started living with Javier did she lose the last vestiges of her panic. After her encounter with Miguel Angel, Elena decided to tackle the problem and overcome her trauma. With a keen and demanding eye, she shopped around for someone suitable to deflower her and coldly and calculatingly chose one of her professors. He was a forty-year-old warm and affectionate man, an experienced man who was very gentle a few weeks later in a roadside motel on the outskirts of Madrid, in a place famous in those years of strict morality for closing one eye when registering suspicious couples with nonexistent identification. Even today, nine years later, whenever Elena takes that road and glimpses the distant silhouette of the motel among the factories and industrial pollution, she remembers losing her virginity and feels a little older each time.)

It is still too early for the drugstore to seethe with the sinister air of nocturnal strays, but the bar has already been taken up by the perennial night owls: lonely men looking for young flesh, old men with dyed hair and silk scarves who strain to keep their flabby paunches sucked in. Elena heads straight for the food counter, gets some milk, maybe I should pick up something to eat—ham, cheese, sausage, bread, something quick and easy—there's nothing in the house and I'm starving, who knows if Javier will come home and feel like eating. Gloomily she thinks what a disaster she is at keeping house, even worse at sharing one, perhaps I'm only good at being a lover. She has lived by herself for years, too many, and her little quirks have developed into full-blown obsessions. You've turned your surroundings into an extension of yourself and learned to live in chaos. Elena is sure that her ineptness at compromise has helped wreck her relationship with Javier; she feels him to be an intruder who barged into her home and robbed her of her space—space in her closets, space on her work table, space for herself. She is so caught up in her routine as a single woman that she perceives any change as a personal attack, a threat to her independence. So, little by little, their foolish quarrels have turned into an outright aggression that poisons their days, their friendship, their love.

Her one year of living with Javier has disabused them of all illusions and filled the air with destructive, useless words. As their relationship crumbled, sex became a painfully automatic act for her. And for Javier? No, surely not for Javier. He was the one who, every night without fail, searched for the warmth of her thighs, regardless of the evening argument, the all-day bickering, the anger, as if one could separate sex from the breakfast he had so impatiently demanded that morning. Javier is a man accustomed to being waited on by women; he has a long personal biography filled with mothers, sisters, solicitous wives. It is just that today—I can't figure out why it's precisely today and not before—Elena sees it as an attack on her freedom. Such are the miserable skirmishes of living together, the battle of the coffee cups.

They used to run into each other at the university at the start of the academic year. Elena was a lowly instructor; Javier, a brilliant young full professor. She was tickled by him from the start, attracted by his bungling ways, his crumpled sport coats threadbare at the elbows, his cheerful baby face, and that mane of tousled curls that drifted behind him. He had the reputation of being shy and absentminded. He misplaced something every day—a pen, a grade book, an appointment calendar, a test file, a scarf or umbrella, his wallet at a bar or his watch in the bathroom. And he blushed easily, which made Elena melt because, like Ana, she had come to the conclusion that only men who were able to blush deserved to be loved. Javier was a tall, slender man who nevertheless belonged to that body type that spreads out from the hips down into sluggish heavy-set legs. Indeed, he lumbered around like a tipsy sailor, and curiously enough, this contributed to his offbeat charm.

They had exchanged little more than greetings the few times they had seen each other, when Elena, under some feeble pretense, decided to invite Javier to a quaint restaurant for lunch. Hardly touching his food, Javier rambled on wildly and incoherently, while she patiently awaited her chance. Elena was a woman who knew how to charm and when to take the initiative. "I think," he stated matter-of-factly, "that all remotely intelligent people are monogamous—sequentially monogamous, that is—and that goes for me too, of course that goes for me too." Elena could recall the blond silhouette of Javier's wife, whom she had seen once on campus. They had been together seven years and had one son. "I myself am monogamous," he insisted, "and I don't believe there's a viable alternative."

Meanwhile Elena was forcing down a mouthful of stew and wondering, then what in the hell am I doing here? "But Javier," she answered, "I also consider myself monogamous, but I've never been in a situation to prove it." "Why's that?" "Because somehow I always get stuck being the other woman. I seem to keep falling for men who are either married or living with someone." "Bah," Javier is adamant, "that won't get you anywhere, that's a dead-end street, aside from being shallow and absurd." And Elena certainly felt idiotic throughout this exchange and mentally kicked herself: I sure have a brilliant career ahead of me with this man, was I ever wrong about you. Nevertheless, after dessert she invited him up to her place for a cup of coffee—"it's right around the corner"—and he immediately accepted. Javier plopped down on the couch and talked incessantly, either about his department or about his theory of scientific monism. He was detached, almost lecturing. After listening to him for half an hour, Elena decided to go for broke. She leaned over and interrupted his dissertation with a quick peck on the lips and a nervous laugh: "After all you told me at lunch, I don't know why I'm doing this but anyhow . . ." Unperturbed, Javier continued explaining the dialectical links in so-called reality; for twenty minutes he developed his thesis without so much as twitching a muscle, impervious to that light kiss that was neither innocent nor casual. ("Can he really just ignore it . . . not even a mild reaction?" Elena wondered, growing more disheartened by the minute.) Suddenly Javier uncoiled his long arm and wrapped it around her neck. "Give me a kiss," he said, drawing her to him. They made love right there on the couch. A month later he left his wife and moved in with Elena—when she saw him standing at her door, nervously clutching his suitcases, she was both overjoyed and terrified. By that time, Elena was very much in love. Javier was tender, naive, affectionate, and his face took on an astonished look during orgasm. "Can it be this good? I just don't believe it," he would say later, blushing like a teenager.

The house is empty, Javier is still not home even though it is nearly eleven, and in fact Elena is relieved. At twenty-eight, she sometimes feels that life has passed her by, that she is about washed up and has lost her youth and tenderness somewhere along the way. Even the disintegration of her relationship with Javier—so sudden, so matter-of-fact—surprises her by being so devoid of pain. Elena is dejected but dry-eyed. She just feels thoroughly drained, convinced that their break is definitive and irreversible. It is the same sense of exhaustion that she felt when she dropped out of the Communist party. "*Les suivants sont toujours plus volontaires,*" some poet said, and Elena agrees: the next time around always takes an act of will, the next loves after the first, the next hopes, the next trust. When you are very young, love and dreams catch you by surprise, overwhelm you, sweep you away, leave you helpless and baffled by such powerful emotions. Then, little by little, year after year, it takes an ever greater act of will to care, to keep on caring; you must force yourself to feel, to fall in love with a man or with an ideal. The next time around . . . Elena is now living the next after the next after the next—and she is worn out from the struggle.

"Hi."

Javier has just come in, sullen, disheveled, and listless, a folder tucked under his arm. The air is still charged with the morning argument, an invisible tangle of little hatreds. He paces the floor, clears his throat, digs into the pocket of his trench coat. Finally he goes up to Elena and, without a word, clumsily and timidly sets on the table an innocent-looking triangular carton, a carton of milk that without any doubt will taste like tears.

Four

Ana is taking advantage of the weekend lull to have a leisurely breakfast at her neighbor's apartment. Ana María is a shy woman pushing forty with granny glasses perched over her introverted smile. She tries to camouflage her sweet face and wears a protective cover of perennially somber clothes—dark corduroy slacks, masculine bulky sweaters—as if she were afraid that someone might notice her soft feminine curves beneath the shapeless woolen contours. They put on some music, make toast—these breakfasts have become a ritual, an alternative to the usual domestic drudgery.

"My, my . . . what's this?"

On the table a jar of Nescafe doubles as a makeshift flower vase. A dozen withered roses display their drooping buds like rotten stumps suspended from long stems. Ana María blushes and stammers, "It's . . . it's a present from that jerk who, well, who stood me up the other day. We were going to meet at some restaurant and he never showed up, and what do you know?—the next day he sent these flowers and a note saying, 'Sorry I couldn't make it, I'll call you Monday,' that sort of stuff." Ana is amused; "nice touch," she comments ironically. "The only thing though," continues Ana María shamefacedly, "is that of course he didn't call . . . not on Monday or Tuesday or Wednesday, I tell you he's a real bastard."

Ana María is a doctor. She and Ana met some months back when their mail got confused and was delivered to the other's apartment, an understandable mixup, since they have the same first name and live on the same floor. From that day they have been very close, like sisters. It was Ana María who helped her through the dreadful morning when Curro woke up burning with fever, paralyzed and delirious, when Ana was convinced he had meningitis and thought she would die from the pain, overcome by a sorrow and fear unknown to her until then. It was Ana María who rushed the child to the hospital, who speeded up the emergency lab reports and the boy's recovery. Ana has been indebted to her ever since.

"They were . . . ," Ana María is saying in her indecisive voice, "you know, they were such pretty roses." She seems to apologize for her words. "Hell, why deny it, I'm a hopeless idiot! But somehow I hate to throw them away."

"Better face it, one day you'll have to. They're turning my stomach, it's like having a dozen mummies on your table."

"Yeah, yeah, I know. It's just that no one's ever sent me flowers."

"Me either."

Ana María is meticulously spreading butter on a slice of toast, painstakingly touching up the edges and smoothing out the bumps with surgical care, as if it were a matter of life or death. "It's just that we . . ." she continues, delicately dipping the tip of her knife into the butter, "we're the kind of women who always thought of it as bunk, the flower bit I mean, and we've always dated men who felt the same way." Ana agrees, "Right. That's why getting roses at this age turns your head. I wouldn't mind it myself." Ana suddenly recalls that she was given a beautiful gladiolus when she turned seventeen. The boy was kind of dumb and terribly old-fashioned, and to top it off he had the nerve to tell her that the flower would last longer if she put it in the refrigerator, can you imagine the absurdity? He thought it belonged between the chicken and the fish, and the thing to do was to open the door and peek at it whenever you wanted to smell it. The two women laugh it off while Curro spills chocolate milk all over his pajamas. He is gulping it down as usual, and it drips off his chin.

"Speaking of bastards," Ana perks up, "guess who called me?"

"I give up."

"José María. You know, my ol' standby. Ever since I got him out of my system, he does nothing but call. It's unbelievable, you'd think he was doing it on purpose—but no, he now seems more hooked than ever. And you know what? I haven't said a word, he must sense I'm turned off, I mean . . . yuk!"

Ana met José María right after her twentieth birthday. He was close to thirty, self-assured with a brilliant mind, a caustic tongue, and an ironic wit that disconcerted her and kept her off guard. At the time she was just a kid, still a virgin, and José María was living with a woman to whom he was more or less faithful. So Ana admired him from afar. Later on he disappeared from Madrid, just about the time Ana gave up her virginity in less-than-spectacular fashion—with a friend to whom she had said nothing and who was too drunk to even notice. When José María turned up again, she fell head over heels, and for years José María, his wife, and Ana dragged out a difficult and listless triangle, each one aware of the situation and trying to play it cool. They had a tacit agreement that he would be the one to call the shots. Ana bent her schedule to his timetable, to his needs, so different from hers that she ended up exhausted. She eventually broke it off out of boredom and self-preservation. Ana tried to maintain a friendship with José María and had other affairs, but for the longest time she found herself seeking out traces of her first love in the ones that followed. It is now and only now, almost ten years later, that Ana feels truly liberated. She woke up one fine day, a morning apparently like any other, and realized that José María was no longer a source of pain. From that moment on, he has redoubled his phone calls, and his voice has taken on plaintive tones.

"No, no, don't, please, don't! No!"

The half-buttered toast is forgotten on the plate, Ana snaps out of her daydream, Curro jerks his head and asks, frightened, "What's that?" while Ana María raises a finger to her lips signaling for silence. They sit listening to the screams that have started up again and are coming through the floor. This is the first time that Ana can distinguish any words in the confusion of moans. "You know, of course," whispers Ana María, "my apartment is right above theirs." The three of them cringe in silence and concentrate on deciphering their neighbors' groans, their pained cries. "That's a woman," Ana comments after a while. "Yeah, that's her," Ana María answers. "What do you mean 'her'? Aren't there two girls downstairs?" Ana asks. "Two girls and one pervert. I don't know what they're up to, but it sounds like a massacre." Five minutes go by, ten, fifteen. The supposed beating keeps up and, in sinister flashes, takes on a certain fanfare. At other times everything goes quiet. Finally they hear, as if it had been held back, a sustained tortured groan. There are moments when the floor seems to buckle from the blows and the stomping. Ana and Ana María get up, follow along the floorboards in pursuit of the exact scene of the alleged crime, as they label it amid bouts of nervous laughter, trace the sounds from one room to the next. Now they go toward the living room, now they are louder in the bathroom, now they crackle just beneath them in the dark corner of the hallway. Their neighbors' apartment is the scene of a senseless and incomprehensible battle. At last the racket dies down, and the air is left reverberating in silence. "Whew!" Ana María lets out a sigh. "I don't know what those weirdos are up to, sometimes they turn loose at three in the morning." "At first," Ana comments, "I thought they were making love—you know, thick in the throes of passion and all that shit—but they've really gone overboard. It's really a sick way to make love." "Make love? What on earth are you talking about? You heard the racket. They're mashing one another to a pulp!" Ana María sums it up, disgusted with the whole thing.

44 Ever since the new neighbors moved in, a man and two women in their early thirties, the days and nights have been spectral with those hair-raising, incoherent screams. He is clean-shaven, with a boyish face, long blond hair, and lanky legs stuffed into tight-fitting jeans. The women are quiet and cheerful; one is dark and wears an Afro, her hair full of split-ends burnt from overperming; the other is tall and angular with limpid eyes. Ever since the new neighbors moved in and began their howling, Ana has tried to come up with possible explanations that were at first logical and soothing but became progressively convoluted and demented. They must be making love, she told herself; and later, they're horsing around; and later still, so they are fighting; after that, when she heard a woman's shrieks, he's hitting one of them. But which one—the small defenseless dark woman or the tall long-suffering one with the watery eyes? Or maybe he's beating them both up. Finally, considering the rage and the thoroughness of these regularly scheduled thrashings, considering the ever longer duration of the wails and the ritualistically slow tempo—"Has it dawned on you that there are never any arguments?" asked Ana María, "that you only hear one girl moaning? That with all the blows, all the commotion, you never hear one peep out of him?"—Ana has even begun to imagine that . . . riiing! . . . at that very moment the doorbell sounds. Ana and Ana María freeze. Finally, Ana María gets up and opens the door. It's him, the neighbor, all innocence and courtesy with a twinkle in his honey-colored eyes. "Excuse me, may I use your phone? It's kinda urgent, I'll only be a minute." Ana María steps back mute from the doorway. He comes in with a grin and dials a number, "Hi, yeah, it's me, yeah . . . yeah . . . I need that guy's address . . . yeah, OK, what was the number again? . . . I got it. From seven to nine, right? Great, thanks." When he hangs up, he turns toward them, "Y'see, I'm out of work, and a buddy has offered

me a gig as a sound technician in a recording studio. Anyway, I gotta check in with that guy this afternoon." The man remains standing in the middle of the room, looking them over with his splendid smile. Ana and Ana María and even Curro stare back icily, trying to discern on the cuffs of his threadbare sleeves some bloodstain, some rip, anything, some definitive proof of their fears and suspicions. But he is already out the door, after thanking them profusely, and they are left amazed and speechless. "You know," Ana finally ventures, "I think that he must be in cahoots with one of the girls, and that they're torturing the other." The idea is so wild that they both burst out laughing. "Which one would you guess to be the victim?" Ana María asks. "I'd go for the one with the perm," Ana responds. "Nah, don't bet on it. She looks like she's got a wild temper. I'd go for the other one. Despite that austere sharp look of hers, she's in the clutches of those two lunatics." Still laughing, they clear away the coffee that by now has gone completely cold.

It is late and Ana has to get to the office. Since there is no day care on Saturday, she has to take Curro along. It will be the usual uproar, with Curro scurrying between the desks, pinching her co-workers, and sucking on their typewriter keys. She looks at herself in the mirror—her hair is filthy, and she has no time to wash it. She feels ugly, and this infuriates her. That's dumb, yeah, a dumb and insecure way to react, but ever since she has been hung up on Soto Amón, Ana wants to look her best for work, even though she is certain that he does not notice her. She is like the schoolgirl with a crush on her teacher who primps even though she suspects that her beloved's eyes will not find her among forty girls in uniform. Ana thinks a lot about Soto Amón, with whom she has yet to exchange a word. It all began as sort of a game, but it is gradually turning into an obsession. She invents him, she dreams him up, she recreates him. She yearns to figure out the hidden man in him. She collects anything that he appears in—magazines, newspaper clippings, even the Senate reports that quote his weighty speeches. She knows the year he was born, how many children he has, the date of his wedding, when he graduated from law school, his first law firm, when he got into the publishing business. Ana pays rapt attention, while feigning indifference, whenever anyone talks about him.

Men in the public eye have an aura about them, and there are always name-droppers who like to brag about a supposed familiarity with the rich and famous . . . and to tell stories that can be far too intimate, far too indiscreet.

"When I was a foreign correspondent in Oslo, and Soto Amón came up for the International Conference of Young Executives, the very first thing he did was to ask me to get him a hot chick, one of those deluxe, Nordic call girls."

Ana doggedly collects outrageous details about him, absurd unrelated tidbits: that he carries a Moroccan coin in his pocket for good luck, that he has a fetish for expensive whores, that he is allergic to flowers, that he was a monarchist as a kid, that he now smokes an occasional joint. Who is the real Soto Amón, in whom so much love and so much hatred converge? Ana prefers to think of him as tender and contradictory. The men she knows—rubber-stamp liberals and late-night swingers—hide beneath their blow-dried hair styles an exasperating iciness, a fear of commitment and confrontation. Perhaps Soto Amón, so appallingly conservative and rigid, is covering up an affectionate, sensitive character and a tantalizingly shy streak. She is well aware that this love is pure make-believe. But so what? Are not all our loves—except perhaps the first one—simple castles in the air? It is possible that in light of daily disenchantments, I feel the need to invent a romance, to rediscover the sparkle of the schoolgirl crush on the teacher, to convince myself I'm still young, to spice up my tedious existence, to forget that I'm thirty years old and that life is escaping swiftly, banally, toward the death that we all carry inside.

(Take for example the death of Concha, her paternal grandmother, that monolith of a woman, very strict and religious. When Ana got pregnant, her grandmother disowned her, banished her from the family,

street corner is once again occupied by old folks, always different yet always the same—the same wrinkles, the same frightened eyes. Downtown Madrid: pollution, noise, traffic, the air thick with soot and dust.
48 No matter. There they are on that pathetic bench that tilts to one side, basking in the poisonous rays of the urban sun while all around them the city shakes from the roar of the buses. There they sit for hours on end, not talking, just satisfied to be together again, hoping that on the following day no one will fail to show up for the unspoken appointment. Only by observing others can they persuade themselves that they are still alive. The old folks on this particular bench look taken care of—their coarse shirt collars are frayed from washing, attesting to the hand of a dutiful daughter. But there are others. There are other types of old men and women: the loners, the drunks, the homeless, the human rags huddled on subway steps and wrapped in newspaper, holding out purplish hands covered with warts, panhandling who knows what besides money, the city's anonymous ghosts, the regulars of some street corner until one cold and damp morning they disappear forever. And there are others still. There are also the classy old gents who do not give up without a struggle. They wear expensive suits and sit on the board of directors until the son-in-law kicks them off or the son replaces them more or less diplomatically. They resort to strolling along the paths of Retiro Park, propped up on antique canes, struggling to maintain a failing dignity. They usually etch a pensive look on their faces to show that their time is still worth something and that they still have important matters to ponder. Whenever they pass a teenage girl with firm flesh, they glance back with watery eyes—the aged are quick to tears and to other sorts of wetness—and take on a childish expression which, in contrast with their decrepit faces, seems more like a monstrous grimace. And then there are the rich old ladies. They still dye their hair and corset themselves in vain. They may dress in black and attend church in search of a skyhook for their fears. Or they may wrap themselves in expensive furs and, with equally rundown friends,

drag their swollen legs along the shopping streets and buy their grandchildren useless hankies at bargain prices. They sip tea in the cafeterias of department stores and talk of backaches and neuralgias, especially of neuralgias. There are also the old fools, those who talk to themselves and wave their arms in the air, those who go out to buy cigarettes or to attend Mass and lose their way, forgetting where they came from and where they were headed. There are hags who dress up like little girls. They wear anklets and stocking caps in the middle of summer and carry empty shopping bags. With failing sight and trembling hands they have smeared lipstick across their mouths and onto their flaccid cheeks. And there are geezers who cross sidewalk cracks with little hops to avoid bad luck, or those who refuse to turn corners out of fears dredged up from their childhood. Then there are the old fags, the flabby queens with sagging moth-eaten skin, who smell of talcum powder and leer sidelong, teary-eyed and crestfallen. And the stumblers, fat matrons who collapse with a dull thud and lie sprawled, quietly moaning until someone gets together enough passersby to lift them to their feet. There are rickety wisps of men who fall to the ground with the sound of bones cracking. And still others. Old men and women with the look of death beneath their eyelids, whose parched skin allows their all-consuming sickness to show through. They stare out of vacant eyes and tremble at the lips, perhaps afraid to betray their imminent departure. They inhabit the world of the living as if they still belonged, but each carries a death sentence stamped on the brow with remarkable precision: this one has only a few months left, that one will not live to see spring, the one over there will be dead in two weeks. They let off a warm pungent stench, the smell of urine and the grave.

Cecilio is in the habit of saying, "One day we'll die foolishly, slipping and bumping our head in the shower, dying slowly, for hours on end, with no one expected to stop by on a regular visit, our weak voice will go unheeded and we'll end up in the newspapers, the corpse of an old man has been discovered . . ." Cecilio, under any circumstances, has a definite tragicomic, melodramatic flair, a tendency toward histrionics. Perhaps his loneliness is more acute, surrounded by all those unattainable young men. At forty, middle age is beginning to make his flesh hang in insidious folds. His yearning for love, in which he no longer believes, is slipping through his fingers like exciting adolescents who disappear, leaving no trace.

"Do you realize that there is a glut of people living alone in the world? Each day there are more and more of us. Sad, isn't it?"

That is what Cecilio often says, and that is what he said the last time they got together, on Tuesday . . . or maybe Wednesday, anyway two or three days ago. They went to a movie, taking advantage of Curro's visit to his grandparents, and had coffee later at some trendy and hideous downtown bar. "What's more," Ana answered him, "living alone is unhealthy, you end up weird." And Cecilio, "You at least have Curro"—as if that made much of a difference, Ana said to herself, and out loud, "It won't last long anyhow, Curro will leave home, for his own good." But Cecilio kept it up: "Still, he lightens the loneliness a bit. You know I can already picture my own old age. I'll be an eccentric, fear-ridden little old man, drooling hopelessly over the young boys of the future. Can you see me? I'll be feebly pining away for some callous youth who is yet to be born . . ."

Listening to him that night after the movie, saddened by his words and loving him dearly, Ana repeated a private joke:

"OK, when we're too decrepit to make it on our own, we'll get married, how 'bout that?"

"Perfect," Cecilio responded without letting go of his obsession, "the news caption will read—the corpses of an elderly couple were found, both showing advanced signs of decomposition."

"Enough, enough."

Tuesday or Wednesday night, they were sipping their last cup of coffee, and a young man came over to wait on them. His long hair was demurely tied back behind his ears, and his meager body was encased in the oversized red jacket of his borrowed uniform. The anything-but-casual glance with which Cecilio so thoroughly sized him up, a contrived leer steeped in insinuations and overtones, immediately let Ana know that this last-minute coffee would go on indefinitely. "Oops!" Cecilio exclaimed, "I've knocked over my glass, I'm so sorry." The boy fumbled for a rag at the bar and returned smiling, a bit flustered but self-assured at the same time. "Don't worry about it, sir, no problem at all." Cecilio was insistent—"No, no, let me help you"—and the boy, embarrassed, emphasized his refusal with an adamant shake of his head: "No sir, really, please don't bother."

"When do you close?"

"We get out at two, well, we close at one-thirty, but by the time we clean up and all . . ." As the waiter moved away from the bar, his jacket rippling on his slight shoulders, Cecilio turned toward Ana beaming.

"That was an obvious come-on."

"You think so?"

"Of course, I only asked him what time they closed, and he answered when they would get off . . ."

It was twelve-thirty, they had finished their coffee, the last dregs were cold, the ashtray was filled with cigarette butts, the entire scene announced that the party was over. "So what happens now?" Ana asked. "We'll wait, of course. What a question, haven't you ever been picked up?" Ana had to stop and think about it: well, it's true, it had been so long that she forgot. And besides, standard heterosexual flirting can be so very predictable. "But," Cecilio added in an upbeat tone, "the gay come-on is always risky, kinky, it's a gas."

The flirtation was just taking off. They ordered more coffee, extra sugar, ice water, while the men exchanged meaningful glances, sultry smiles, open dares. Then the lights started to flicker, announcing closing time, and an older waiter began scrubbing away the grime that rose like an island chain across the counter. The young man took off his jacket and rolled up his sleeves, exposing the downy hair on his tanned forearms. ("What is this? A public striptease, just like that?" "But I have to clean the coffee maker, sir.") Cecilio's slow gaze deliciously feasted on the blanket of adolescent fuzz that covered the boy's already sinewy and

virile wrists, on the glowing warmth at the nape of the neck, dazzling yet half hidden by his collar.

They were finally kicked out of the bar at a moment when the boy was out of sight, perhaps lost in the kitchen. They climbed into Cecilio's car and parked on the corner with the headlights off and the motor running, "just in case there's a chase." The street was deserted at this late hour of a cold spring night. They passed the time smoking and making disconnected small talk, but at some point Cecilio dropped his voice to a confidential whisper. "I can't really explain it, but at times I feel so despondent that . . . I go out, I see a boy I like who brushes by me, totally aloof, unaware of me and joking with his friends in that crude grownup way that these kids put on . . . I see someone like that pass right by and disappear behind me, and I feel almost a jolt. I get morbidly depressed because I can't call him back, because I'm losing him, because I'll never see him again to tell him that he excites me—no, Ana dear, I'm not talking about fucking him, it's not that—I don't know if I'm making any sense. What turns me on is not the idea of making love to him but a puzzling, sensuous, affectionate feeling."

Suddenly they came out, all of them at once. The cook, the older waiter, the manager, the kid, the cashier. They waved goodbye at the door and split into groups. The boy and the two men went up the street and disappeared into the dark. One could barely make out his mod leather jacket and the sway of his faded jeans stretched tightly over firm buttocks. Cecilio took off after them and, in one minute, broke every traffic rule in the book. He sped through red lights, made U-turns, and under the cover of darkness drove down pedestrian lanes. He saw them turn into a one-way street. "We'll follow down the next one and surprise them from behind, I'll go easy." He almost ran them over at the first intersection, where the wheels of his car miraculously just missed their feet. The car was going so slowly and the street was so narrow that the near-accident on that dark corner seemed more like a rendezvous, a salute. Cecilio went mute, and through the window Ana could see the gloating expression on the boy's face, a barely hidden malicious leer of triumph. It was impossible to catch up with him again; he ducked into some side street where the night engulfed his blue jeans. Ana and Cecilio hardly spoke as he drove her home, and Ana now knows that they will never mention the downy softness, the fleeting glow of that young boy.

Curro is furious at Ana because she did not let him wear his little leather jacket, the one covered with punk zippers that he feels so handsome in. Ana thought it was too cold and, in a fit of maternal zeal, stuffed him into the red and blue parka that he hates. So now he is in a rage and having one of those colossal tantrums that he knows how to store in his tiny body. Since getting off the bus, he has kept three paces behind Ana, as if flaunting "I don't know that stupid woman." When they turn the corner, however, two things happen. First, a huge dog, a monster with a hairy square snout, tries to sniff Curro with obviously friendly intentions that Curro misinterprets. So putting aside his pride, given his disadvantage in size, he runs avidly and helplessly to clutch his mother's hand. Second, from a distance, they see a commotion in front of the offices of the *News*: patrol cars with flashing lights, and helmeted policemen officiously waving their arms amid a throng of bystanders. It is not quite clear whether mother or son is more desperately clutching the other as they quicken their pace and join the crowd. Some look tense, while others crack jokes. Romero, the illustrator, greets Ana with a wide grin. "No big deal, they've planted another bomb, the usual. They threw us out of the building, and now they're conducting their little search. Delightful, isn't it?" Ana is distressed—what a day to bring the kid. Curro is strangely silent and well behaved, keeping a grip on her hand as if sensing that something out of the ordinary is going on. Marina, from the newspaper staff, sexily brushes back her long hair and leans down to say, "My, what a beautiful child! Is he your son?" As she straightens back up, she seizes the chance to give Ana a poorly disguised once-over, an avid glance that sizes Ana up from head to toe. Marina is the type of woman who has to scrutinize and make mental notes of other women's clothes. It is an ingrained habit that Ana despises. "Let's see how long this takes, what a hassle," Ana comments just to say something. In the crowd she notices Mateo waving. "Do you have the article?" "Yeah, sure." "Good, if these guys ever finish, we can look it over," Mateo answers in a shrill voice. The atmosphere is a cross between a wake and a picnic: it is the third time they have evacuated the building, and people are beginning to take it lightly. Yet there still lingers in everyone's memory the tragic and bloody death of two colleagues at a competing magazine where a bomb recently did explode. In the corridors one still hears: "When was it that *Today* . . ." "Three months ago, no, maybe four." "The bastards . . ." Although no one says any more, everyone recalls the exact details, the front-page photos of the mutilated bodies with their hands ripped off and their stomachs gutted, the walls splattered with slabs of flesh. Awful. Over there, a few steps to the right, are the VIPs: Domingo the managing editor, Luis Barbastro the editor-in-chief, and Soto Amón. Marina is now eagerly spreading some in-house gossip in hushed tones: "Have you heard the latest?" "Yeah, we've just had a bomb scare," Romero answers. "Don't be an ass, I'm serious." "OK, enough," Ana intervenes, disgusted with the secret ritual, "what is it?" Marina smiles complacently, thrilled to be the one to break the news: "Just that Sánchez Mora left his wife and moved in with Pili, you know the one who works in management." Ana shrugs her shoulders. "He can do what he damn well pleases for all I care." A police officer comes out, talks to the executives, and they motion that it is safe to go back inside. OK, let's go, cross your fingers that they searched every nook and cranny.

While Curro chews on staples and bangs on the keys of her neighbor's typewriter, Ana proofreads her draft:

". . . a generation of men now in their forties, born at the end of our civil war and brought up with all the overblown rhetoric of the triumphant crusade, is now going through its midlife crisis. This so-called lost generation now holds positions of authority; this brilliant generation now governs Spain but is beginning to feel on shaky ground. Perhaps everything these men believed in was a lie, their entire life a sham. The ideals they fought for are now questionable and, hiding behind the lapels of a perfectly cut suit, behind ties of Italian silk, they have a vague sense that they may have been cheated. The directors, the executives, the presidents, the entrepreneurs of our national destiny are now lighting up their first joints and, through the smoky haze, are seeing the outlines of a different age . . ."

Sánchez Mora. Sánchez Mora has come into the newsroom while Ana is putting the finishing touches to the article, and she thinks that he epitomizes everything she has just read. There he is across the room, as pudgy as a Buddha, a fortyish, well-dressed prig, his puffy round face aglow with joy and madness today. Because he must feel reckless, overjoyed and downright insane, to have risked such a step. Because Sánchez Mora is prim and meticulous, a cagey corporate man, a quiet yes-man, a loyal wretch cowed by authority and discipline. He married quite young and has a large family. According to the grapevine, he used to be ultra-conservative, a member of *Opus Dei,* but just a few months ago switched to the Workers party. Sánchez and Pili, that lump of a secretary, so young, so provincial, so overfed. This paragraph exactly fits the stamp of the adulterous director of the *News*. Like a glove, Ana thinks, although she wrote it about someone else, about the enigmatic Soto Amón. Unable to approach him directly, since he is the top banana, Ana has taken to sending him coded messages, making him silent offerings, writing him intimately couched SOS telegrams in the vain hope that he will catch the true gist of her words, their hidden meaning, with the naive goal that Soto Amón will read those messages and understand, that he will find her, that he will know her. Ana feels like the schoolgirl who lovingly fills in the margins of her homework exercises with clumsy sketches of little flowers, amorous doodles dedicated to the teacher who will correct them.

". . . Power carries with it castration, an irreducible binary. Sexual repression under Franco was no coincidence: it was aimed toward sublimation for greater productivity, toward a stricter adherence to the rules. It was the sexual sublimation of an entire nation as buttress for one man's self-aggrandizement, a reflection of the castration at the highest levels of government. The so-called sexual revolution inevitably must affect first those who were the principal victims of the power structure: these postwar Spaniards now in their forties. Mostly men—women are a case apart; they were not offered power in exchange for sexual repression but were used to shore up the male power structure—men who now find themselves married to women they never wanted as companions, with grownup children who are total strangers. In short, those desolate middle-aged men who are now forced to admit that they have been accomplices to their own emotional castration, in exchange for which they have conquered the dragon, the paper dragon."

A paper dragon like Soto Amón's. And so, week after week and month after month, Ana strains to invent new literary deceits, to implant intimate messages published in all-apparent innocence, the private jokes of her imagination and her desire.

". . . and so, if we take as a case in point a man, let's say, born on August 29, 1935 . . ." At least he'll be surprised to see the exact date of his birth, Ana says to herself with her hopes up.

"Ana, dear, this is all very fine," Mateo says with that cordial plastic smile he puts on whenever he is ready to criticize or call someone on the carpet, "but all you journalists have a habit of editorializing that drives me up the wall . . . Look, hon, why don't you just give the facts, I mean, do more true reporting, and let the readers draw their own conclusions?"

Of course Ana knows that Mateo is right, but how can she explain why she must defend her inflated prose? How do you admit that these passages are unaddressed letters to an unreachable man? So she ends up arguing with the editor-in-chief, having to placate, to promise, to fight for every inch of these lovingly elaborated phrases.

Between one thing and another, the bomb included, Ana arrives late as usual to meet with Pulga. Curro races after her, grumbling because of her quick pace, "Mommy, don't run so fast." They finally reach the entrance of the flea market, and there is Pulga impatiently puffing on a cigarette, as tiny and androgynous as a flea herself, with close-cropped and curly auburn hair and a pug nose awash in freckles. It can't be that Pulga is already thirty-three; she looks like a teenage tomboy. "Oh, Ana, you're hopeless," she grumbles as she grinds out her cigarette with the spike heel of her boot. (Pulga has a shrimp complex and is always tottering on unbelievable stilts.) "I'm sorry, Pulguita, but I'm just now getting off work, someone planted a bomb." "Someone planted a what?!" They leave the explanations for later and go into the market. It is almost closing time, and Pulga wants to splurge on something, anything, since her affair with Chamaco in particular and life in general is not going too smoothly. Every time she gets depressed, Pulga is overwhelmed with an insatiable urge to shop. The vendor stalls glow like a lit-up Nativity scene, motley clothes hang from the rafters, and on the tables there is an array of bizarre objects—miniature glass elephants, midget-size satin purses, costume jewelry, jars of patchouli, inlaid wooden boxes, little tin Chinese bells. Curro knocks over a rack of scarves while trying to swing from one like Tarzan. Pulga announces that she wants to buy a skirt—you in a skirt?—yeah, I'm tired of always going around in jeans, it's hit me that I want to feel feminine. So they go around to the back and Pulga tries on one skirt after another, a black one with white flowers, a patchwork blue one, another one with flounces. She finally collapses into a chair and wails in desperation, "It's disgusting! I'm such a runt, nothing looks good on me." The truth is that Pulga usually shops in the boys' section of department stores, since those are the only clothes that suit her diminutive figure without need for alterations.

She finally buys a sweater and a vest and admits, "I always end up with the same stuff." Now with her packages in hand and beginning to feel guilty for the useless expenses, as she always does when she shops compulsively, Pulga drags Ana and Curro over to the bar across the street where she has agreed to meet Chamaco. The bar is called the Immortal but is a sinister and decrepit spot where diverse and hostile decors clash, beginning with the walls that started out green but have peeled and faded to a putrid yellow. The marble-top table has a broken leg, there are some rickety chairs of wood and formica, and the obviously new counter is made of cheap acrylic. Half the neon lights are burned out, the back mirror is mottled with flyspecks, and on the counter several platters are half-filled with petrified food that resembles moldy tripe and vintage liver covered with dust and clotted in grease. The place is deserted except for an old man in a well-worn jacket who is chomping on a cigar. Behind the counter stands a young woman with a horsy face who seems crippled and somewhat retarded. Above the coffee machine, on a wall calendar, smiles a now blurred but still voluptuous Brigitte Bardot look-alike with bouffant hair and enormous breasts spreading across the photograph; the date is 1967. Ana wonders if there is anything more pathetic than an old calendar, desolately useless, exhibiting with foolish pride its worthless pages that no one bothered to turn.

"What a bummer of a place," Pulga shudders. Just to be safe, they order two Cokes and a Fanta and, even so, have to wipe off the smudges from the glasses while the waitress opens the bottles with exasperating deliberation, concentrating all her mental energy on the task.

"Hey there."

Chamaco comes in, cheerfully strutting on the high heels of his cowboy boots, wearing tight jeans, a bomber jacket with a fake leather collar, and a black T-shirt with a tiger on the chest.

"Wow, Chamaco!" Ana blurts out. "That's some haircut, I wouldn't have recognized you."

"Compliments of the army."

Chamaco had a case of stomach ulcers that exempted him from military duty the first time he was called up. But now, at twenty-three and thanks to Pulga's culinary and maternal pampering, he is completely cured and can no longer avoid the draft. "Just this morning, he had his picture taken," Pulga explains, "soooo . . ."

Chamaco raps on the counter with his bejeweled knuckles, "Hey, bring me a scotch, will ya? And I want the real thing." He flashes a wad of bills and boasts, "Today I'm paying." Pulga looks alarmed. "Where'd you get that money?" she asks. "Bah, a little here, a little there," he answers evasively, "none of your business." "What d'ya mean, none of my business? C'mon, tell me, where did it come from?" And Chamaco gloats with superiority, "Look, Pulgui, don't be such a pain in the ass. You're always hassling me to make some bread, right? Well here it is, so fuck off." "Chamaco, don't be a fool, you're asking for big trouble." He finally strides over to them and confidingly pulls out a little square packet wrapped in tinfoil. "Here's where it comes from, and it'll keep right on comin'. I'm selling hash for a friend, and I'm gonna score big. Hey, what's the matter with you two?" Pulga just stares daggers at him and says after a pause, "You know, Chamaco, you're a real jerk. They'll catch you pushing that shit. And to top it all off, now that you're in the service, you'll end up in jail, like an idiot." He shrugs, "Ah, get lost," snatches up his drink, spins on his heels, and heads over to the pinball machine in the corner—bing, bing, boing, boing, bing, bing, bing, boing, boiiing—the racket does not let up until the contraption swallows his coins.

Pulga sulks over her Coke in embarrassed silence. After a while she leans toward Ana and whispers, "Listen, don't mention this to Elena, OK?" Ana assures her that she will not breathe a word.

It so happens that Pulga is scared of Elena; their relationship is turning into that of naughty child and critical parent. Pulga looks up to her because she thinks Elena is more intelligent and better educated, but at the same time she dreads her acid wit, her superior tone, her critical attitude. Elena, she thinks dejectedly, sees me as dumber than I really am. Maybe she doesn't realize that in many ways she is a privileged woman. She got to go to college, have ambitions, make the most of her time. Pulga, however, was the middle daughter of a penniless family and had to drop out of high school in her third year. Her first job was as secretary for a filmmaker, and little by little she worked her way into public relations with a powerful multinational distributing company. Her job can be considered enviable: hobnobbing with the rich and famous, lots of travel, lots of contacts. But her career has also given her a fast-track frivolity. She lives for the present in fictitious luxury, spends her nights getting loaded with casual drinking buddies, and improvises scintillating friendships that dissolve the next morning into headaches and hangovers. Pulga lives at a high-speed, chaotic pace.

When she married at nineteen, she had barely been around: some parties, a few stolen kisses and furtive passes. He had just arrived in Madrid, an aspiring actor, and it took him quite a while to make the right connections. They met, they liked each other, and in six months they were married. Pulga came to her Church-sanctioned honeymoon bed a frightened virgin. He raped her wordlessly, clumsily, and painfully; the next morning she woke up with her pillow drenched in tears and a tight burning between her legs. "A type of vaginitis" was the doctor's tentative diagnosis. Later, after the tests and lab reports, he confirmed it and specified, "Psychosomatic." She and her husband never had sex again nor made mention of that first night. They shared the same roof for three years in a tense, enemy ceasefire atmosphere. Then they separated, and it was only much later, when Pulga was twenty-seven, that she managed to overcome her fears and try again.

Chamaco keeps on playing pinball, Curro dips his finger in soda and draws invisible sketches on the marble tabletop, and Ana is muttering something about same-ol'-Jose-María, as she calls him, all in one breath. Pulga is having a hard time understanding Ana's words—"just think, after all that's happened, he's still calling me, and now he's begging me . . ."—so she lends a deaf ear, wrapped up as she is in her own problems, mentally recalling the strange bedfellows she has chosen over the past five years, amazed at herself for having gotten involved with Chamaco, that weird crude kid absorbed in his game, his back turned to them. The old man with the cigar is telling the cripple some complicated story that she hears with vacant, mongoloid eyes: "Well, this year, we spent our vacation on the Costa del Sol—Málaga, Torremolinos, the works—it was fabulous," the old man is saying, and Pulga recalls that first it was Esteban, the architecture student whom she helped move out of the apartment he shared with some friends and into hers, where she supported him for a year; then came Francisco, still in his early twenties, who wanted to be a star; she promoted him along and fed his narcissism, and they lived together for almost two years. "So whenever I get time off, I grab the old lady and my jalopy, and we're gone the same day . . . you know, the first thing we do is toss a coin to see which road we'll take, and for the rest of the trip we just flip heads or tails to see where we end up, and so every year we spend our vacation in a different spot." One can overhear the old man as—bing, boing—the pinball machine clatters away. And then there is Chamaco, street-smart Chamaco, whose amazing talents range from being a drummer in a rock band to playing professional pinball. Bing, boing. "Ever since the old lady and I decided to take off like that, on a pure fluke, we've been really living it up." The fact is that Pulga has been choosing younger and younger lovers, each more inexperienced than the last, boys easily star-struck whom she can manipulate. At times, when she starts thinking about her preferences for malleable adolescents, Pulga senses that there is something basically warped with it all. Bing, bing, boiing. "I won a game!" Chamaco flashes them a triumphant smile.

Five

Ana is late again, delayed as usual for some silly reason. (Her chronic lateness sometimes frightens her, and in a fit of metaphorical melancholy she tells herself, "I'm forever late and I'll continue to be late to everything in life, self-confidence included.") When she rings the bell at Julita's house it is already eight o'clock, damn it, even though she had sworn to be early to help with the birthday party. She had promised Julita to come with time to spare, meaning time to listen to her complaints and to dry her tears. Julita opens the door enveloped in the warm smell of burnt sugar. She is drying her hands on her apron; her hair is pulled back in a bun away from her prematurely aged round face. She wears a desolate expression, a sort of childish sadness so apparent lately. "Oh Ana, I was afraid you weren't coming, I'm so glad to see you." They go into the kitchen, and Julita puts the final touches on the cake, finishes arranging the sandwiches on the tray, and distractedly accepts compliments about how yummy everything looks. She moves quickly, obviously eager to get done and sit in the small cluttered den to talk before the others arrive. Julita's eyes are naive, sad, and young;

they are her best feature, those limpid eyes devoid of malice, those permanently perplexed eyes that always seem to be asking something. Today she is made up with more care than usual and has wrapped an Indian skirt around her softly rounded hips. She is on the short side with abundant curves, an innocently fleshed woman. Now, finally sitting down, she puckers her pale round face into a sob. "I feel . . . I don't know," she says choking back her tears in embarrassment. "Oh, Ana, I feel lost, as if everything were coming apart, I'm just overwhelmed with fear," she moans, defeated, no longer trying to hide behind a shaky smile. "I'm so miserable, Ana, I hurt so much . . ."

Today Antonio came by to see the children, and yesterday's precarious balance has come crashing down in tears. Of course it must be hard, very hard, to break up with the man you've lived with for fifteen years, your first lover, your husband. And with three almost grown children. And in a house that is brimming with his presence. And when you have no other identity than that of being his wife. Ana can well understand Julita's pain, but she is fed up with her weeping. They have been separated for almost six months, and for almost six months Julita has been regularly bemoaning his absence. She is like a broken record. For almost six months Ana has been listening to the same words, drying identical tears. She is ambivalent about this relentless repetition, torn between helplessness and plain detached boredom.

"I hate to drag you into this again, Ana, I feel awful," Julita adds, struggling to swallow the tears.

"No, no, don't worry about it, don't be silly," Ana hears herself say and is immediately ashamed of her hypocrisy. Ana knows that she is shy and overly friendly, a friendliness born of insecurity, of the adolescent need to be well liked by all. As Candela used to say, one of the most difficult things to learn in this life is how to deal with others' dislike or with their hatred. When we are children, we want everyone to love us because we realize our weakness. A sign of maturity is learning to accept calmly the impossibility of fulfilling that wish, acknowledging the existence of grudges and enemies. And in this respect Ana is still so immature that she feigns an interest that she is far from feeling. "It's only normal to feel scared at the beginning," she tells Julita, "but give it some time, in a while you may just figure out that the separation has been a boon. Look at your . . . how old are you?" "Thirty-seven." "Well, then, at thirty-seven, with your children almost grown, you'll be able to live like you never have before." But she is well aware that she is just spewing hollow words.

"Ohhhhhhhh . . ." Julita moans shamefacedly, the mascara that she put on today in a self-conscious birthday effort streaming darkly down her cheeks. Ana is silent, not knowing quite what else to do. It is getting dark, and on the jammed bookshelves across the room she can barely make out a photo of the happy couple, a smiling picture of Antonio and Julita ten years younger—he clean-shaven and in a tie, she confidently resting her absurdly fashionable teased hair on his shoulder. Today Antonio looks better, even more handsome with his long beard and loose sweaters. He started smoking pot four years ago and quit the Communist party four months back. When he left his wife, he also broke with his long, illegal, painful history of militancy. ("He is one of the orphans," Elena concluded. "I was lucky to spend only a little time in the party, at least relatively little. I was lucky to belong to a new generation and fight under different circumstances, but those poor bastards who have spent fifteen, twenty years believing each and every Marxist dogma are now strung out, confused, broken.") And so Antonio wanders about a little crazy, rather stupefied, anxious to live and to be young, allowing himself to disagree with the chairman of the party, but only among old comrades, while still maintaining a quiet and furious pride when the criticism comes from outsiders, from those who are not and never have been militants. In other words, he argues with everyone and keeps his dissatisfaction mostly to his solitary self. Antonio now believes that he is in love with a girl ("She's not even pretty," grumbles Julita, "he just couldn't allow himself the frivolity of leaving me for a prettier woman"), and he loves her precisely because she is young, because she is free and independent. He loves in her exactly everything that he helped smother in Julita. "Go ahead and work, if that's what you want," Antonio used to tell her years ago, "go ahead and work, Julita, you know it's all right with me. But you're the type who talks a lot and does very little, and I'm sure that after all your bitching you'll never really get a job, never . . ."

"Listen," says Ana, "this didn't catch you by surprise, did it? You'd been having trouble for years, right?"

"Oh, I don't know . . . I guess so."

"Fine, then this is the best that could've happened. Things have their own life span, you know, relationships die and the worst you can do is drag them out when it's all over. Going on just by sheer inertia would be truly catastrophic."

(Yes, yes, you're right, Ana, you must be right. Still, it's so hard . . . today Antonio showed up in a new jacket. It's unbelievable how much pain a piece of leather can cause. For years I knew his clothes, his socks, his underwear. And suddenly, his absence becomes tangible in the new pants, in an unfamiliar shirt, in a color he wouldn't wear before. He was so conservative, Antonio, so serious, so uptight. This person who comes in a loud sweater is simply a stranger. How're you doin'? he said. You should get yourself a boyfriend, he said. But I don't want anyone else and I'm not even sure that I can. I feel like a frightened virgin, it's been too many years, I'm a one-man woman, and that's out of date. It's so lonely at night in my bed, Ana, there's too much room for nightmares . . . bad dreams about old age, about lost time, about feeling ugly, inadequate, out of step with the world. Will someone ever desire me again? Antonio certainly doesn't, and it's like an insult, a failure, something shameful. I wonder how he makes love to that girl; I wonder if, in that too, he's a stranger who screws in a totally new way. Maybe right now he's different, eager, panting inside her . . . while his new jacket rests at the foot of the bed.)

"Hey, what's going on? Why are you two sitting here in the dark? This looks like a wake . . ."

Ana opened the door, and Elena's arrival caught Julita by surprise. As the lights go on, she blinks, startled and painfully aware of her teary eyes and cheeks smeared in black. "What's the matter, Julita?" says Elena kissing her hello. "Nothing, nothing, you know me," she shrugs it off weakly. "I'll be right back," and she flees the room carrying her birthday present. Elena glances at Ana and points to her own cheeks as a sign of understanding, but Ana ambiguously shrugs her shoulders and pretends to be absorbed in the task of looking for a record. Elena marvels to herself at Ana's ability to listen to others. It's nothing but admirable, she thinks with a tinge of envy, conscious of her own lack of patience. Elena is well aware of Julita's dilemma and can rationally understand the situation. But she herself has never been married, has never lost her own identity, has never allowed herself to be dominated by a man. So she feels very uncomfortable when confronted with a flood of tears, as if Julita's feminine pain triggered some kind of guilty denial and created an almost unbridgeable gap between them. They are so different, and Julita is painfully boring as the distraught little housewife, saddled with a ridiculous and humiliating diminutive perfectly suited to a homebody, who looks for the right detergent and recommends it to all her friends.

By now the doorbell does not stop ringing. There is Cecilio with his latest fling, a cute young boy with an air of self-sufficiency. Then Candela and Pulga arrive, and after them a slim girl with twitchy, unstable shoulders, very quiet and pale. "It's Marisa," explains Julita, who has returned after restoring her makeup to flawless perfection, "she is an old friend of ours . . . I mean mine and Antonio's." For a while the place is abuzz with greetings, kisses, the rustle of colorful giftwrap. "Oh, how nice, thank you," Julita says over and over, looking slightly dizzy while fresh ice cubes clink and the long-forgotten record player has come to a stop.

"Help," Cecilio blurts out at some point, "someone get me a scotch. Quick, I'm a wreck."

And he collapses into a chair with a deep sigh. "What's with you?" asks Julita, and gets only a vague wave of his hand for an answer. "He's lovesick," Ana points out with a twinkle in her eye. "Tell me about it . . ." cracks Julita, managing a contorted smile verging on tears.

"You? Lovesick?" Elena cuts in sarcastically. "Oh, come off it, Cecilio. You guys are immune."

"Cut the crap, Elena," he snaps back. "You should know by now that such generalizations are meaningless."

This riles Elena. She had said it jokingly but now just cannot pass up the challenge. "OK, granted, it's stupid to generalize, and besides you certainly are not the typical macho man. Still, because of upbringing or whatever, you men tend to handle relationships differently than women do." Cecilio protests, denies, gets furious. "That's a damn cliché. I'm fed up with all these empty words like chauvinism and feminism. And you, Elena, are much too intelligent to swallow this thing whole anyway." "But listen," she insists, "men are used to having their own way in relationships; that's why there are so few real friendships among men, have you ever noticed that? And when it comes to friendships with women, well . . . what I mean is that a man always looks out for himself in a relationship, while a woman gets lost in it." "That's a lie," Cecilio answers. "The truth is that all couples are unfortunately one-sided; there's always one who gives and one who takes, which in no way means that women are always the martyrs and men always the tyrants. The roles are perfectly interchangeable." Elena rages on, "It just so happens that in ninety percent of couples it is the woman who gets fucked over, the one who gives herself completely, the one who gives up what she likes and submits to the man while he takes advantage of the situation and gives nothing." At this point Ana jumps in: "It's disgusting how we were brought up that way. Do you remember those books that we used to read as teenagers, like that *Diary of*

Ana María and Daniel? Remember how Ana María's volume was subtitled 'Giving' and Daniel's 'Loving' . . . who knows what the hell that was supposed to mean." Elena adds, "Right, Ana, exactly, and with that kind of shit they tried to teach us our assigned roles. Women were meant to give—in other words, to give in. Men, of course, were meant to love: that is, to forgive, to guide with a soft paternal hand, to shine at the center of creation." Cecilio has started to laugh under his breath. "What absolute nonsense," he mutters, "when you two get going like this there's no way to carry on a halfway lucid discussion."

"I almost agree with Cecilio," pipes in Candela, who has been quiet so far. "I guess we can all get caught in the trap, and the problem is that we don't realize it. There's an infinite gulf between men and women. What's so sad is that we believe in our roles even more than in our true selves . . . well, I feel kind of silly saying this, Elena; after all, they're your own words."

Elena shrugs it off with a smile, "I guess so, surely that's how it turns out. In fact, my article deals precisely with that . . . it's just that I can very rationally understand it all, but when it comes to gut feelings I don't believe it; deep down I'm filled with resentment toward men."

(And Elena thinks about "Odd and Even," the brief essay she is writing about social roles, about a world of stereotypes and opposing categories. She thinks about the difficulty of being single and odd, the difficulty of escaping traditional roles. And she remembers that she is very far behind in her work. "I want it in two months," her publisher said just this afternoon, and Elena knows that she will deliver it in draft form, unpolished, and she's infuriated with herself and with her newly acquired star status. Her brilliant paper at the young philosophers' convention in Burgos and the fact that she is a woman have turned her into this year's celebrity; her name is mentioned among the initiated; she is invited to collaborate in respected journals, to participate in colloquia and lecture series. There is something false and disproportionate in the suddenness of her success, as if just for being a bright, competitive woman in a male-dominated field she had been chosen as mascot for the team and placed above criticism, and now she feels on display like some kind of girl prodigy. This offends her deeply but also flatters her; that is just where the danger lies.)

The others are playing charades and Marisa, the pale girl that no one knew, is crouched on the floor going "cluck, cluck, cluck" as she flops her wiry arms about. Her cheeks are red, almost feverish with excitement and she is beaming. "Hen, a hen!" shouts Julita. "Yes, whoring like a hen!" adds Cecilio triumphantly, and everyone laughs and applauds the winner. Cecilio hugs the young boy with the turned-up nose, who has gotten lost in the confusion. Julita covers her smile with a chubby hand, her eyes so sad that for a moment it is impossible to tell whether she is laughing or crying, and Pulga is oddly quiet just sipping her drink. "Is anything wrong?" Elena whispers. "No . . ." But Elena insists, "Where's your drummer boy? Is he with a baby sitter?" Pulga blushes and gets even smaller. "We don't go out very often these days." "Amazing," Elena almost hisses, "I haven't seen you alone in years, it's the first time that you are not lugging a boy around like a rash on your back . . ." Pulga's silence gets thicker, but Elena is unrelenting: "I can't believe you're through with Chamaco, must be that he lost his charm when they clipped his locks for the service—just like good ol' Samson—and have you picked out the next cradle to snatch yet?" Pulga looks morose, takes a long time to answer, and finally mutters, "No, no, Elena, I've had it with boys, I want to be alone for a while." Elena ends her attack with a sharp and incredulous "about time."

Pulga is acting strange indeed. For once not taking up her usual role as court jester, she has kept to herself all evening long, which is unheard-of for her. Today she is depressed because she has noticed the shanties.

Pulga lives in a new development on the outskirts of Madrid where she rents a highrise apartment, landscaped with imported grass and surrounded by high walls. As she was leaving this morning she got her first glimpse of them. During the night someone had knocked down part of the back wall, and through the hole she could see a barren field littered with garbage and refuse, a field of shanties. Pulga has been living there four years in semiluxury, next to a kind of poverty that she did not know existed, and only today did she become aware of that galling filth, that urban sore which the city takes pains to hide. She is appalled by her discovery, reeling as if the ground had suddenly collapsed under her feet. It is by now a familiar anguish that floods her with intimations of disaster each time reality gets in her way and rears its ugly head. Her life—so public, so glamorous, so glittering—is full of black holes in which everything spins, and it is precisely this void that she attempts to fill with her reckless affairs, with those naive boys that she pampers and collects.

Now, since things are not working out with Chamaco, Pulga wants to turn over a new leaf in her life; she wants to get used to being alone and adult. The trouble is that her days are mined with black holes, and her nights unravel in strange and awful noises. She has to tiptoe around ever so cautiously in the dark, barely breathing while her heart is pounding wildly in her chest, always afraid that around the next corner she might confront horror itself, that dark core hidden by daily life, the same way she found the unsuspected shanties behind the garden wall.

Suddenly there are shouts coming from the dark street, and Pulga is startled, her slightly paranoid tendencies stirred. Julita opens the window. Javier and Roberto, the pale woman's husband, are yelling to be let in. The woman gets up, hastily quitting the game of charades: "I'll get the door," she says. "Never mind," answers Julita, "I can just throw them the key wrapped in a handkerchief." "No, no, I'll go," the weak-shouldered woman insists, taking the clinking bundle and running downstairs.

Roberto starts complaining at once. He has been down there for half an hour because he lost the phone number and could not remember the floor; fortunately, this guy arrived and started to yell. " 'This guy' is Javier," says Julita, beginning with the introductions. "This is Roberto." "Hello, hello." Roberto is a rather short man with pronounced cheekbones and a thick mustache who moves around with a smug smile. Following him, always at a discreet distance, is the pale woman now smiling silently, and Ana, seeing her appear and disappear behind her husband's shoulder as he walks about, thinks that she seems to be crouching, that she now looks tense, almost shrunken.

Javier has taken a plateful of sandwiches from the table and sits next to Elena wolfing them down. Well, she thinks, he's pissed off; she has learned to pick up his moods from the twist of his mouth. "I'm starved," he says rather gruffly, "Damn," he adds with disgust, "this one's paté, d'you want it?" Elena shakes her head no and watches him intently, waiting for the showdown. "What's with you?" he finally bursts out. "With me? Nothing," she answers, "you're the one who seems uptight." He does not reply at first, concentrating on chewing furiously, but finally he snaps, "I waited for you at home for two and a half hours." "For me?" "Is that all you can say today?" "But why did you wait?" "We'd agreed to come together, remember?" Javier barks back, all the while looking out of the corner of his eye toward Candela who is sitting nearby observing them. "That's news to me," Elena says, feeling her anger rise. She is briefly tempted to start one of their endless arguments, but the whole thing seems too ludicrous, and she makes an effort to soften her voice. "Hey, don't be silly, I said that I had to see my publisher today and that since it's so close I would come straight over." Javier is quiet at first, perhaps even remembering this conversation, but then he insists again with childish stubbornness, "You know very well my car's in the shop; the least you could've done was to come and get me, I'm really beat." "And I'm pretty tired myself, you know," she snaps back angrily but then adds, "besides, you could've come directly from the university instead of stopping by the house." Javier's face is twisted. "Leave me alone," he mumbles and walks across the room to sit sulking at the other end.

Javier said, "Leave me alone"; he almost yelled it as if he really meant it when in truth he cannot do without her. In the last few months Elena has been choking on this dead-end affair, yet there she is, still locked into the rut and gasping like a fish out of water. In an attempt to save herself, and whatever is left of their love, she tried to talk Javier into separating for a while, living in different houses, trying to have a more open relationship; but he does not believe in such solutions and is forestalling the inevitable with feeble excuses. First it was a bad case of the flu with a protracted convalescence that kept him from leaving, and now that he is back on his feet he seems to have forgotten all about that argument, fakes a life-as-usual attitude, and avoids dangerous encounters. Elena wonders if she will ever get rid of him. There is something of an arrested childhood in this man who left his parents' house to marry and then left his wife to move in with her. He has always been cared for and pampered, has never been totally independent. And so he is insecure. Insecure about his ideas, about his political allegiances, about his beliefs, about his profession—all the more so now with Elena's success, which he experiences with a painful, ambivalent mixture of pride and jealousy.

(Last Sunday, Elena recalls, they had dinner with his parents, a very traditional couple, narrow-minded and ultra-right-wing. Javier picked a fight with them, worked himself into a frenzy debunking their simplistic ideas, betraying a stubbornness typical of teenagers, and Elena realized that he was attempting to make the break postponed since adolescence, to make the break now, so late, so crudely, at thirty-two.)

The party chatter is growing thin. Candela has left to pick up her children, Javier is locked into monosyllabic anger, Cecilio and his boy have taken off for their nightly cruising, and Roberto is engaged in some talk about his work—engineering? . . . geology? . . . what the hell is he saying about oil platforms?—something very specialized and pedantic to which Julita listens patiently. To his right, quiet and different since his arrival, her sunken cheeks once again pale, is his wife Marisa, who now does not participate; she simply occupies space mutely, motionlessly, keeping her thin hands crossed limply on her lap. It is time to go.

Elena and Javier exit quickly, wrapped in a cloud of resentment. Ana, who is very sleepy, would have liked to do the same, but at the corner Pulga suddenly insists on going somewhere for a last drink. Pulga is never eager to go home; she always tries to stay as long as possible, just a few more minutes. "C'mon, don't be such a drag, Ana, for once you are free of Curro, hey, let's have some fun."

So they wander over to their friends' pub, Galáctica, a cramped place with thick foul air, which is jammed as usual. "Ana, such a nice surprise!" says Mercedes, one of the owners, from the other side of the bar. "Long time no see." They kiss warmly, and Ana notices that sweat is pouring down Mercedes's face. It is sweltering in there. "I don't wanna hear it," says Tomás, Mercedes's husband, who comes to greet them, "the air conditioning broke down but the beat goes on." Mercedes is looking good, young and radiant at forty. She has clipped an enormous mauve feather to her curly, graying mane and has poured her slightly excessive curves into a purple velvet dress. "Listen," Mercedes leans over the bar, her face suddenly serious, "have you seen my son lately?" "No, not lately, why?" "Well, he hasn't been home in three days." "Doesn't he come around here either?" Tomás shrugs his shoulders and looks hurt, "Around here? Ha! that horny little brat doesn't set foot in this place." Ana doesn't quite know what to say; she feels uncomfortable in the role of go-between with which they have saddled her. Finally, since someone next to her is asking for a vodka, she sees a way out, utters some trite words of consolation—don't worry, it's probably nothing—and excuses herself. She joins Pulga at a hard-fought-for corner table, won in battle against a moon-eyed girl and some little twerp with an earlobe full of earrings, perhaps in compensation for his shortness.

As soon as Ana sits down, Pulga pulls out a meticulously rolled joint from under the table. "Let's get high, huh?" she says. "Sure, go ahead," Ana replies. "You light up a cigarette too, so it's not too obvious." Ana gets one of hers, a white-filtered look-alike. They set the chipped ashtray in the middle of the table, and they smoke slowly—one drag on the joint, one on the cigarette; they put one down and pick up the other in a real dance of hands and fumes. "This shit's not so hot," Pulga boasts knowingly, "it's just straight Moroccan green, but I'm about to score some sinsemilla." Since she got involved with Chamaco, Pulga has changed a lot; her speech is peppered with drug terms, and it seems that at thirty-three she has turned into a shallow, swinging dopehead. Poor kid, thinks Ana. Pulga is always looking for shelter in others, always surrounded by friends and noise, filling the dead hours, the emptiness, stumbling through life trying to find a niche for herself. She was frivolously Marxist when she was with Esteban, the architecture student; when she dated Francisco, the aspiring actor, she learned to quote Artaud, Piscator, and Grotowski—never having read anything by them, needless to say; and now with Chamaco she is completely spaced out. Poor Pulga, undefined and aimless. "There's a terrific new bar, we've gotta go one of these days," she says, "but actually where I like to hang out is at Tony's, an old place that we've taken over." Ana hears the cozy pride in that "we." "I know Tony's, Pulga, all too well," and cuts off her spiel with a tired gesture; after all, she vividly recalls her insane nights there, with the same cast and backdrop.

It has been a long time since then, since Ana has frequented the "in" spots. She quit the bar scene when she got tired of wasting her time in such raucous loneliness. In those days she would hang out with her childhood friend Olga, her confidante about early boyfriends, her job-hunting buddy, the same Olga who fell madly in love with Zorro and who, later on, took off for India. Olga chose to drop out, while Ana stuck to the nine-to-five routine. It's been so long since I've heard from her, I miss her, thinks Ana with an acute attack of nostalgia. Through the bluish haze Ana picks out familiar faces, old friends left over from that wild time of entire nights spent dreaming up ambitious projects, carving out the future with Olga in whispers. Over there is Patitas, his polio limp more pronounced with age; a bit further is Mora, heaving her drunken body on the table; and in that other corner the Baron and Músculo are leaning against a back wall painted black with fluorescent

stars. Pulga chatters nonstop, and Ana pays no attention while she sips her tea and lets her mind drift toward Soto Amón. Suddenly she smiles to herself; here we go again, both locked into our own obsessions: me with the usual and Pulga trying to be amusing with her stories just to postpone going home alone.

There is a commotion, a few gasps, someone bursts into applause, and Zorro makes his grand entrance, his enormous frame outlandishly decked out. He is clad in satin harem pants and brocade vest, his feet are filthy and bare in spite of the cold, and above his thick black beard shines an eye heavily made up as a butterfly in greens and blues and purples. "Wow, look at Zorro," urges Pulga needlessly, as if his presence could possibly be overlooked. "Yeah, yeah, look at him, he gets weirder by the day." Zorro walks about with a fixed, dumb smile; as he gets closer, Ana notices his bloodshot eyes, how he leans on the backs of chairs to keep his balance, "he's totally smashed." He crosses the bar with the satisfaction of being the center of attention, greets the chosen few, and finally, standing in the middle of the pub, yells in a thick voice, "OK, who's gonna buy me a drink?" "Aw, go on, you've had enough," says Patitas, shrugging his shoulders and looking at Zorro's muscles with clear envy. "You guys are cheapskates," complains Zorro, still smiling. He takes a plastic gun from the toy holster slung on his hip: "Bang, bang," he shoots, "you're dead, all dead, you're all dead meat." Someone hisses, Zorro stuffs his gun away clumsily and whips out a knife, which he brandishes with an air of triumph. Then he proceeds to open it slowly and awkwardly in a ripple of nervous giggles. "C'mon Zorro, that's enough," Mercedes is mumbling behind him as she tries to grab him by the arm. But Zorro lets loose and swings right and left as if doing a magic trick, "nothing up this sleeve, nothing up that sleeve," he says and with a jerk he cuts the veins of his left wrist. "Holy shit," someone yells amid panicky screams. "What a bloody fool," says Pulga, her voice a mere thread. Ana amazes herself by calmly observing the mother-of-pearl handle of the blade. Zorro stands a full head taller than those who have gathered around him; he is laughing with an empty roar and, waving his slashed arm high above, sprays everyone with his blood.

(Elena and Javier rode all the way home without speaking and now, already in bed, Elena hastily grabs a book and scowls to better define the limits of her indifference. Javier slips under the blanket and stares at the ceiling until he finally lets out a desolate, endless sigh and murmurs a barely audible "sorry." Just watch it, Elena is thinking, next he'll want to fuck. "Sorry," he repeats a bit louder, "I just don't know what's gotten into me lately, Elena," and he turns toward her a comically contorted face. "Now I'll try to make love to you, and you'll hit me over the head with the book. Damn, what a mess." Elena cannot help laughing a little. "That's exactly what I'll do," she tells him as Javier, encouraged by the apparent thaw, tries to hug her. "No, wait, Javier, wait, that doesn't solve anything. Wait, let's talk a little," but Javier ignores her words, teases and tickles and finally penetrates her. Elena receives him dejectedly, without desire, almost absently. Javier's erection is playful, if a bit precarious, but then he loses it and ends up sobbing. "Hold me, please, keep me inside you," he mumbles, his voice breaking as he buries his tearful face in her shoulder, "keep me inside you, please, I'm so lonely." It is the first time Elena has seen him cry.)

Six

It is that difficult lost hour of dusk, when it is always too early or too late for anything. On the work table a long overdue project awaits, but Cecilio feels itchy and unable to concentrate. In the summer Madrid becomes sweaty, dirty, sticky. And exciting. He has not been out all day; in a surge of will power he made up his mind to lock himself in and work. But of course the hours have flown by, the project is still stalled, and Cecilio has not even eaten because there was absolutely nothing in the refrigerator. Perhaps his upset stomach is partly to blame for his dejected mood, for the disabling afternoon slump. His upset stomach and the several scotches he has already downed. The Concha Piquer record has come to a stop in the growing darkness, and the last few sad notes of "Tatoo" still float in the air. Her records are one of his most private vices, the kind that no one admits. Concha's romantic songs take him right back to his childhood; as a postwar baby, Cecilio was weaned on the melodies of Bobby Deglanne. Forty years old. He is already forty years old. Unbelievable. He was still young not so long ago, and now he is rounding the last stretch. It seems like yesterday when he roamed the streets of his desolate whitewashed village, that two-bit town lost in provincial Jaen where he was born. Those were times of hunger, of poverty. He lived in an adobe hut with dirt floors, and his mother cried at night. So Cecilio studied hard, won scholarships, used all his energy trying to get out of that hole in the wall. But his childhood was not unhappy. He played in the streets, he skinned his knees, he got into scrapes with his playmates. Or rather, they got into scrapes with him. At fourteen Cecilio was a bony kid, and as pale as if he had been bleached. He was intelligent and hardworking but nearsighted and fearful. His friends—stronger, healthier—poked fun at him and considered him a wimp. Especially Juan, the muscular, olive-skinned group leader who boasted awkward toughness. One day, for some trivial reason, Juan took a swing at him, a mean punch that knocked his glasses off—ol' four eyes, they used to call him, ol' bookworm—and that one time he hit back, who knows why, perhaps he was fed up or perhaps it was something else. Cecilio grabbed him, attempting to stay close to his opponent so that he would not be hit again. He shut his eyes tightly to avoid watching his own recklessness and pounded Juan on the back with a barrage of weak blows from fists not used to fighting. The other boy struggled to break loose and finally threw him to the ground and jumped astride him. Cecilio opened his eyes: the boy's face was close to his, a menacing face with a flat nose and dark, flashing eyes. Cecilio felt a strange sensation run through his body, a wave of pleasure mixed with pain. He lost what little strength he had, dropped his fists, and felt a rush of happiness at his surrender. For an instant they panted together, their breaths mixing, observing each other, discovering something new. Then Juan shot up, suddenly serious. OK, enough, he said with an authoritarian tone as the crowd of gawkers dispersed complaining, you should have bashed his nose. From that day on Juan never bothered Cecilio again, and in fact the group broke up soon afterward when they started chasing girls.

Cecilio too. Every afternoon he would visit Reme, the baker's daughter. She was a bit chubby, with close-set eyes and pointed breasts. She was quiet and affectionate and always smelled of dough and cinnamon; some days she gave him small sweet rolls, hard as stones, that Cecilio would gobble with visible enjoyment. So he went to Reme's at sundown, sat with her in front of the shop, wolfed down his roll to the girl's delight—being somewhat of a glutton herself, she very much enjoyed seeing others eat. ("Cecilio, you gotta fatten yerself up, you gotta study hard so we can get hitched soon," she would say when she was in a chatty mood.) Then they would kiss each other on the cheek and say goodbye. On Sundays they would walk up and down the road holding hands, meeting other couples. One afternoon, during the town festival, Reme danced a lot and seemed particularly excited, given her usually placid temperament. Dragging him to a darkened corner she asked him, "D'ya love me? d'ya love me?" And he, somewhat frightened, said yes, he did love her. "A lot? a whole lot?" And he could only repeat, "Yes, lots, lots." Suddenly Remedios leaped on him, dug her breasts into his chest, kissed his lips. "Reme," he mumbled very scared and trying to get away, but she took his face in her strong, sure hands and held him tightly. She pressed him against the wall and searched inside his mouth with her tongue, a tongue that Cecilio found salty, cold, and slimy, a tongue that disgusted him.

Soon afterward he left town. He was nineteen and wanted to continue studying. He left to go to Madrid, a place that seemed like the end of the world, the land of promise and countless vices. He arrived at the south train station one morning with only a few pesetas to his name, his eyes heavy with sleep after the uncomfortable night journey, and a cardboard suitcase in his hand. As he left the station, cars sped chaotically past him, people rushed to work. Before him he saw a huge billboard advertising aftershave. He looked at it with fascination, his suitcase on the ground, his hands in his pockets. And it was there, at that precise moment in front of the ad, that the truth surfaced with a calming certainty: "Damn, I'm gay," he realized. And immediately felt intensely relieved.

Now that Concha Piquer has finished and the fourth scotch is giving a wobbly, physical dimension to his melancholy, Cecilio recalls that Ana is about to go on vacation. In a flash he is overcome with a great urge to see her, he needs a friendly companion to launch the barely begun evening, he is eager to experience something surprising and beautiful. Nights are deceitful, he reflects—booze awakens his philosophical streak—they always promise more than they deliver. But no matter, Cecilio is in the throes of those first enticing hours in which everything seems possible and the fresh darkness brims with adventure. So he dials Ana's number: "Hey, let's go out awhile, have a few laughs, say goodbye. Take the kid to his grandma's, I'll pick you up around nine-thirty."

The first thing he said to her was his classic opener, "Let's go have a drink," slurred through an already thick tongue. Ana agreed, noticing that he was smashed. And so now, with the oppressive heat turned into a summer shower, Cecilio and Ana navigate against the rain in search of the dimly lit haven of Duetto across the street, a half-open door that lets out beams of amber light.

"Well hi, Cecilio. What hole d'you crawl out from? I haven't seen you in ages."

"Right, hello. Well, you know, work and things like that . . . have you met Ana?"

"Did you ever finish that amphitheater project?"

"Which one?"

"That contest at the Costa Brava or wherever . . ."

"Ah, yeah . . . it was in Almería. Yeah, I finished it. I mean, it's already built."

"Man, that was fast. So, what can I get you?"

It takes him a split second. He wants another scotch, of course. His still empty stomach is scarcely warmed by the previous ones. "I'll stick with scotch, Tony." It must be the fifth or sixth or . . . actually, what he really craves is a steak. A steak with fries. With pimentos. With a glass of good red wine and bread, too. Fresh, crunchy bread. But needless to say, Cecilio must wait for his someone special to show up. Ana observes her friend. She knows full well that this outing is not haphazard, that they have come to Duetto because of an unspoken date. "I'll have an orange juice," she says. "You are moderation personified," hisses Cecilio in a display of knee-jerk aggressiveness that Ana simply ignores.

"What was that, Cecilio?"

Tony leans over the table, struggling to be heard over the loud music.

"Nothing, I'm just kind of drunk."

"Yeah, what else is new."

"You can skip that. Listen, have you seen Morritos around?"

"So that's what it is . . . you're still hung up on him."

"No, not really . . . I just want to give him a message."

"Yeah, all right, a message. Well, you're a big boy now, it's your business how you waste your time. And actually, yes, he was here and left a while back to go to the movies with Angel. I think they said something about coming back later on, so if you wanna hang around you can catch him then."

"I'll do that."

"As I said, you're a big boy . . ."

So that's it. It's Morritos's spell again. That forbidden, evasive boy that Cecilio had been crazy about. Ana thought he had gotten over it. Actually, she knows that his obsession is all make-believe, a manifestation of his basic need for love. And Ana knows that Cecilio knows it too, which makes it even worse. The artificial air that fills the bar is thick and pungent. In the jumble of heads, shoulders, backs, one can pick out the usual ones: Alain the Belgian, Díez Monter the film director with the rest of his crew, including Marina all glitzed up in an expensive Indian silk sari that delicately bares an unnaturally pale shoulder. Cecilio hunkers down behind his glass and sinks into the cushions seeming slightly apprehensive, letting his eyes wander idly, responding to an occasional wave with a quick nod of the head—an exact mixture of aloofness and courtesy—ignoring Ana or rather just feeling her presence as his anchor to reality, as his lifebuoy. Andreu, looking sinister in a white suit that gives him the air of an apparition in this smoke-filled darkness, flutters by flabby and decadent, table-hopping with a servile smile under his sweaty mustache, his most classic and professional public relations smile.

"Good evening, sir, what a pleasure to see you here again. And good evening to you, too, Miss . . ."

In spite of Cecilio's fervent wish to remain unnoticed, he does not succeed in escaping Andreu's electronic eye. "Must be lack of faith," he mumbles out loud.

"What's that?" the whitish puppet bends over, never altering his smile, a tense grimace that hangs from the well-trained corners of his mouth.

"Nothing."

Behind Andreu's leaning torso there finally emerges the reigning playmate of the month, compliments of the house, open for inspection, tax free. "Oh, there's Alejandro." The boy looks silently at Cecilio and purses his lips, attempting a sexy smile that shrivels into a crass smirk.

"Hey, Cecilio! . . . I'm talking to you, man, where are you?" shouts Andreu.

"Huh?"

"I was saying that I came with a real nice guy. Even though you have such a pretty date"—he smiles unctuously at Ana—"perhaps you'd like to meet some new people. Here, I can introduce you, this is Alej . . ."

"Don't bother, we already know each other. Isn't that right?"

Perhaps Alejandro's tanned baby face is flushing, or it could be just the reflection of the lights from the bar.

"Besides, Andreu, we're waiting for some friends. And besides, I'm very cozy with Ana, just the two of us. And besides, I'm kinda drunk. And besides, I don't need anyone. OK?"

"OK, OK, I get it, don't be so touchy. So, no sweat, I'll catch you later.

Enjoy your buzz and your lovely date"—another obsequious smile in Ana's direction. "But I'm warning you, one of these days you may get lonesome, and loneliness makes for bad company, you know. I was just trying to do you a favor, there's nothing in it for me . . ."

"Yeah, yeah, thanks a lot. Catch you later, OK?"

Shoes well shined, glistening like glass. A denim jacket, a vest in shades of red, gray pants of fine cloth, cut wide with pleats at the waist. His short, wavy hair slicked back at the temples with gel. A splendid specimen, this guy Alejandro, a splendid specimen for sale at the evening meat market. Seventeen, eighteen years old at most, neither better looking nor brighter nor younger than any of the others, those dozens of young boys who populate the forbidden Madrid.

(It was Jaime who had spotted Alejandro at some gameroom one afternoon, that same Jaime who occasionally pimps. Cecilio had never been involved with him, not directly anyway; he had merely seen him again and again, in all the cafés, at all the parties, in all the clubs—that boy is a marvel of ubiquity. He was more or less handsome, more or less well dressed, more or less polite, which put him in that genre of pretentious tramps who do not actually charge for their services, those who prance before the powerful, who exchange sexual favors (with the likes of Andreu) for introductions just so they can offer themselves almost altruistically to the avid hands of high-powered journalists, movie producers, theater directors, television magnates, jetsetters, anyone who could launch them toward stardom. Because Alejandro, needless to say, wants to be an actor, like all the others. He slicks his hair each morning in front of the mirror either at home or in the motel where he ends up; he slicks his hair every morning to perk himself up: you're so good-looking, Alejandro, today is gonna be a good one. Alejandro begins his day very early as jack-of-all-trades in the field of sex. He not only does the evening shift, the expensive highbrow Madrid night, dressed in his best threads with his rebellious locks in place, putting on his warpaint around ten, a good time to start to prowl. No. He also gets an early start in the morning and can be spotted at the downtown movie theaters, at those horny lonely matinees where cheap tricks abound; after lunch he does the gamerooms, and later on, after dark, he starts working the streets behind the main square, Puerta del Sol, where many like him feed their hunger, their desires, their dreams. A many-faceted boy, this Alejandro, and judging from his life-style he is either extremely ambitious or just plain starving.)

So we wait, we sit here waiting for Morritos. Ana silently drinks the sour synthetic brew that passes for orange juice and thinks about these impossible homosexual relations, this tortured waiting game that is the ultimate symbol, the most blatant proof of the trouble in all intimate relationships: the loss of faith in the couple. So we wait. Cecilio, meanwhile, decides to get thoroughly drunk and pursues this undertaking with admirable determination, drowning out the time until Morritos's arrival. Morritos is eighteen, another aspiring actor, how predictable can one get. His hair is blond and curly, his body adolescent thin, his full lips both innocent and wicked at once. Or not. Perhaps his wickedness is also a pose. His face is altogether naive and dull, no more than that, beautifully and sensually dull. Cecilio is completely drunk now, thinking that this is his final love. No, that's not true either, this is just the end of the fireworks. When was the last time that he fell really in love? The last time that hope won over boredom, over the deadly knowledge of everything that would happen, of everything his latest flame would say and do? It has been so long that he cannot even remember. In any case, if this boy is not his final fling, at the very least he is his last encuntment, this macho term being easily transplanted by virtue of his alcoholic stupor to an ill-fitting context. If this is not his final love, then it is the most recent incarnation of his neurosis, his longing for these provocative, unattainable boys.

"Hey there man, fancy seeing you here."

Morritos has caught him in the midst of a crisis of self-pity, feeling ridiculous and decadent sitting there on that beat-up leather couch.

"What d'ya mean . . . can't I have a drink like everyone else . . . ?"

"Go easy man, sure you can, this place belongs to a friend of yours, doesn't it? It's just that I haven't seen you hanging out in so long, that's all. Hi Ana, I didn't recognize you at first."

Morritos bends over and kisses her on both cheeks, "you look great," he winks, wiggles, flirts. "Excuse me, I'll be right back, OK?" he says at last. And turning his back to them he walks away swaying his slight frame gracefully, his half-finished androgynous frame posed precisely on the border between male and female. His soft curls brush the nape of his neck at every step with a narcissistic caress that confirms his beauty. And Cecilio thinks that they are much too beautiful, these boys, much too suggestive and sinister, much too disturbing with their taut flesh and their youth. They use up all their energy to look beautiful, but deep down they are flat, even exhaustingly dumb, repeating each other like clones, perfect specimens of human stupidity. Morritos is talking with Tony, flirting with Alain, laughing to call attention to his gorgeous teeth, to be the focus of all glances, to make sure that Cecilio keeps looking at him and pining away. He has no idea, cannot even begin to fathom how Cecilio cherishes him, how he offers up the best in himself; he is oblivious to the depth and beauty of this secret homage that old fogies like Cecilio dedicate to such unreachable studs.

"God, it's hot in here, huh?" Morritos fans himself affectedly with his hand.

"Mmmmmmmm."

"Well, I'm hot. Perhaps it's because of that mixed drink. Guess I'm not used to them, you know . . . anyway, what's new with you?"

"Mmmmmmmmmm."

"Man, you're weird today, Cecilio."

"I'm drunk."

"You? I don't believe it."

"Fine."

"I've never seen you drunk."

"So now you have."

And Cecilio considers the time he has wasted, the hours spent amusing this boy, trying to dazzle him with his wit, waiting for him, precious lost hours, hours next to a phone that does not ring, so much energy squandered on this prima donna, on the brief bloom of his adolescence, on this piece of meat hollow on the inside.

"Can I have a sip of your drink? I'm dying of thirst."

"Mmmmmmmm."

"Thanks. So, tell me, what've you been doing? Where've you been hiding?"

And Cecilio ponders the blank afternoons awaiting him, the half-finished project on his desk, the doorbell that does not ring, the inability to concentrate in those endless evenings, each minute becoming more interminable with the increasing certainty that he would not come. And he recalls going out late at night looking for him at Tops, where he usually parades at those hours, and feverishly crossing Madrid accompanied by whoever is willing to waste some time. He remembers arriving at Tops and spotting him at the end of the bar with his easy smile, the cheeks flushed by the excitement of flirting, and exchanging two curt words in code with him only to realize that he is playing the fool. It is already 3:00 A.M., and Cecilio is soaked in too much booze, and he knows that the next morning he has to be at work at eight-thirty and that he must be clearheaded, professional, steady on his feet, so he grabs his silent friend by the arm and stumbles in defeat toward the door. He breathes in the cold dawn, feeling the bitter emptiness of his mouth, the too many cigarettes, all those drinks, and his head throbs, but it hurts much less than his soul in any case. And they have to cross a city that is ugly and dark at that time, a Madrid now filled with freaks of all kinds, unspeakable loners at an hour when every passing shadow seems to be selling something. And there is still the hardest trial of all, there is still the raw neon light in the elevator, the damning mirror that reflects your defeat, the bags under your eyes, the forty years that are beginning to plummet down your face, the nicotine-induced late-hour pallor, an insanely mad pallor. This is emptiness, Cecilio, this is emptiness.

"Hey, are you listening? Where've you been hiding?"

"Around."

"OK, Cecilio, you're really weird today. Just tell me if I'm buggin' you."

"No, you don't bother me, I'm just drunk."

"Fine."

Morritos is quiet, sitting on the edge of the table, one leg crossed over the other with a certain flair, eyeing the scene dreamily. Ana, however, is sure that he is taking in every piece of the action.

He gets up suddenly: "I'm cutting out, man, have to meet some people."

"Mmmmmmmmmm."

"Goodbye, Cecilio, *ciao* Ana, be seein' ya."

They are alone again, with empty glasses. Cecilio turns and smiles.

"Ana."

"What?"

"When I turn fifty . . ."

"Mmmmm, you still have a ways to go . . ."

"When I turn fifty, I'm gonna have myself castrated."

"Aha."

"When I turn fifty, I'm gonna have myself castrated, and I'll throw a party for all my lovers and ex-lovers to announce it. And the next day I'll go and have it done. Then I'll live peacefully just working, reading, listening to music while I get fat and lose my hair—I've heard that's what happens when you get castrated—so I'll gain weight, get flabby, go bald, I mean even balder than I am now . . ."

"You'll make a very funny eunuch," Ana jokes, picking up on his festive tone, but she feels worried and sad inside.

"Ha, ha . . . I'll turn into a Roman matron, that's my thing . . . ha, ha."

He thinks for a moment, his mouth open as if ready for more laughter, but then adds with darkened and drunken voice, "Please take me home, Ana, Anita . . ."

Seven

It's a torture, a real torture to have to iron in this heat, Ana is thinking as she feels the sweat trickle down her neck making wet patterns on her back. The iron plops over and over against the table as she presses collars, Curro's pants, shirts, her skirts, plop, plop. Ana can barely lift the iron and makes careless strokes that often catch wrinkles and press them into the fabric. If my mother could see me making such a mess, thinks Ana. She hates it. She hates to wash dishes, or iron, or sew; she hates those dreary domestic chores that eat up her time and make her feel the burden of routine. When she presses the folds of a dress with the burning edge of the iron, she is overwhelmed with boredom, an anticipated boredom for all the clothes that she still has to iron in the next ten, twenty, thirty years. Well, all right. Tomorrow she is leaving on vacation, and there is no other way to get her clothes in minimally decent shape. She has spent the whole day cooped up in her scorching apartment, scrubbing and picking up, watering some plants, transporting others to Ana María's and urging her to pamper them, water them adequately and even talk to them at times so they will be happy and not miss her, since as we all know, plants like music and affection.

The mound of clothes is visibly shrinking, the sun is going down, a light afternoon breeze makes its way in and puts up a fight against the mugginess, and Ana's spirits begin to lift. Suddenly there it is, the usual earthquake: some hushed words, something dragging across the floor, a few quick, rhythmical blows as the ritualistic prologue. Then the sighs that soon turn into moans that turn into cries that turn into shrieks, exasperating, tearstained shrieks. There they go again, the downstairs neighbors doing their thing. In this heat she has all the windows of the apartment open, and so today the echoes of the mysterious happening come not only through the walls but also through every crack and cranny, all the beams and bricks and especially the windows. They get progressively louder and take on agonizingly sharp, terrifying tones. Ana continues to iron, attempting to stay calm and aloof, but the neighbors' pain becomes overwhelming on this hot and sweaty afternoon. She recalls the last time she talked with Ana María about this. (Every time they get together they always end up talking about the same thing. First a quick briefing on the strange behavior of "the beast," as they call the man that Ana María is infatuated with, then a passing mention of Ana's own impossible yearning for her unreachable boss, and finally and unavoidably on to the noises, the screams, the anguish that explode within the neighboring walls.) They considered simply asking them directly what was going on. "But," pointed out Ana María, "what if what we imagine is true? What if there really is a victim who is being tortured by one or both of them? What if our question sets them off and makes them even more violent?" Of course, there was also the fear of ridicule. "Maybe they're just making love . . . the truth is usually a lot simpler than all this melodrama that we're inventing," they would tell each other in saner moments. "Or, perhaps, one of them is an epileptic," Ana ventured once. "Epilepsy? I don't think so," Ana María replied, "but maybe the woman is hysterical and goes on these yelling sprees without any provocation. Perhaps this is her way of torturing the others." "Which one of them, do you think?" Ana would always end up asking, unable to decide herself. "Take your pick, either the one with the glassy eyes or the one with the kinky hair."

(Ohhhhhh, no, no, no, ahhhhhhh). In order to avoid listening, Ana tries to reconstruct in detail Candela's recent visit. She came by to bring Ana a suitcase for her trip, since the handle on Ana's finally gave out in that tumultuous trip to Ibiza last summer. Candela was almost sad, almost dejected, given her proverbial serenity.

"They're going to commit María José, the paranoid girl that I've been treating."

Candela explained that María José was going on sixteen and had been in her care for two years already. She was the fifth of seven children—her father a government employee, her mother neurotically possessive. María José was the weakest in a family characterized by irrational, despotic behavior; she was the most sensitive and helpless, and her relatives had labeled her the crazy one and had made her the scapegoat of their own guilt. Now María José had become a burden to the family, and in a flurry of excuses and self-serving rationalizations they were going to commit her to a psychiatric ward. Just that morning María José had cried, screamed, moaned, clinging to Candela's waist.

(Uhhhhhhhhhh, ahhhhhhhh.) Candela also talked about Pulga and Julita. She had gone out to dinner with them the night before. "You can't imagine how awful they looked, Ana, they were both ashen and puffy, and Pulga even boasted about having gone to bed at eight that morning, about her dissipated life-style. They are like little kids, those two." Since Pulga had broken up with Chamaco and was afraid to succumb to her loneliness, she dragged Julita along, as a sort of satellite to a falling star, and they now spent their time filling each other's emptiness. "Maybe turning loose will do them good," Ana ventured. "I don't know about that" replied Candela. "Seems to me they're as lost as a fish on a bicycle. Being afraid to face yourself can be really destructive, you know." And Ana again: "It's just that you have managed to reach a balance that, from the outside at least, seems admirable, Candela. But not everyone is so lucky, you see, we each have to deal with emptiness the best way we can." Candela was quiet, paced the room, lit a cigarette, and finally said, "That's all I try to do, Ana, precisely and only that. And you can bet that my serenity is sometimes just a smoke screen." "But still . . ." Ana was not sure she could be more specific. "Still," Candela cut in, "I do think that I'm happy enough, I'm fairly satisfied with myself." And she went on about her life at thirty-six, her two children, her challenging job. "When I was younger I tried to grab the moment, you know, to follow the fashion of accumulating experiences, squeezing the present dry and all that . . . in any case, I really believed it and I acted on it, but it was a lie. I was up to my ears in future projects, in anxieties. It turns out that now, without consciously pursuing the present, I'm truly beginning to live one day at a time. Whether it's my house filled with plants, listening to music, reading, talking with my children, whatever, it's all newly charged with pleasure and meaning for me. The change, the big change came when I split with Vicente, Jara's father, remember him? Well, it dawned on me that I was completely absorbed in that guy, that I was trying to skip over, to literally burn up the days when I wasn't with him. Until it hit me that I was thirty. I was horrified to think that I was throwing away my life, not taking full advantage of each and every day. It was a real epiphany, I tell you, a flash—like when you suddenly see the pattern in a puzzle or when the jigsaw pieces finally come together. When this happened, I also realized that Vicente was only an excuse, a way to focus on the future and evade the daily anguish. It's all a simple matter of projecting your desires for happiness onto a man, or onto the hope that you'll win the lottery, or find a better house, or whatever. It doesn't matter what, just so long as it deflects into tomorrow your responsibility to yourself. And I decided I didn't want that, Ana, I just didn't want to keep on wasting my life."

(No, no, ohhhhhhhhhh.) She's on the last shirt, and still the screaming continues. Ana looks at her watch. They've been going at it for forty-five minutes. Two more strokes with the iron and it is all done. She pulls out the plug, picks up the clothes, and puts them on the bed,

next to the open suitcase. She sits for a moment and lights a cigarette. They are shouting. In this lull in her chores the screams sound even louder, or perhaps they are indeed louder. Ana nervously chews on the filter of her cigarette, she is exasperated; this time it is lasting longer than ever. She reaches for the phone and dials Ana María. She lets the phone go on ringing, even when she is sure that her neighbor is not there. She keeps the receiver to her ear, letting the rings muffle and accompany the solitary notes of those screams. "Damn it, that's enough . . . this is really obscene, these people have no right to . . ." The shouting continues unabated. She gets up, goes to the bathroom, splashes her wrists and her temples with cold water while the yelling goes on. Here in the bathroom the sounds are louder than anywhere else; perhaps they come through the vent. Yes, that's where they are coming from, Ana realizes with morbid fascination. She kneels down, brings her ear close to the floor near a tile that Curro cracked with a hammer last summer. The screams go on and on. Now they are sharp and cutting like shards, now they fade a bit, now they almost turn into pained sighs. More blows and then one blow, one muffled moan. Perfect rhythm. "He's beating her, that sonofabitch," Ana says again out loud, both outraged and afraid. With sudden decisiveness she gets up, crosses the apartment at lightning speed, opens the door, goes down the ratty stairs to the floor below and stops on the landing. There is barely any light coming in through the grate at this hour, and it is difficult to make out the neighbors' door, an old, ill-fitting door with a thick coat of cheap, industrial-grade brown paint. Funny thing, from here the sounds are less audible, there's scarcely a whisper way in there, must be a curious acoustic phenomenon. Ana raises her finger in the direction of the bell, keeps it there momentarily but draws back again, lacking the nerve to press the fateful button. The screams seem to be subsiding little by little in the guts of the house. There is a brief silence. Ana wavers. If I do ring, what do I say? That I heard them screaming and wondered whether there was a problem? Whether I can help?

"Hi . . ."

The door has opened abruptly, and the neighbor is standing there looking at her with surprise.

"Were you coming here? Did you want anything?" he asks solicitously.

"No . . . yes . . . it's just that you startled me when you opened the door before I had time to knock," Ana laughs, shaken and blushing.

"Oh, sorry, I was just leaving and . . ."

"No, don't worry, please, I'm on my way."

Ana turns and starts to leave. "Wait," he says, "what did you want?" "Ah, yeah," Ana improvises, "do you have any cigarettes? I ran out and . . ." He goes back into the apartment, where everything is shrouded in a thick silence. Through the door Ana can see stacks of books all over the place. Finally he returns with a half-pack of cigarettes. "Here, I don't smoke, but my friends do. Yeah, you can keep it, we have more." And as they say goodbye, he flashes her a splendid and beatific smile.

Eight

"His face had a sort of pseudofeminine softness, like the softness of a flabby thigh, his sagging cheeks seemed to tumble down his face.

'We won't be hiring until next year but . . . what'd you say your name was, hon?'

'Ana Antón.'

'Antón, Antón . . .' he repeated to himself while he looked distractedly through a list. 'Ah, yeah . . . this is very fine. You did well on the tests. Perhaps something could be done, after all.' He raised his listless, shifty eyes and looked her over with an air of complicity. 'In fact, I'm sure we can take care of this.'

She felt the unspoken demand in his words, as if he expected a certain specific behavior from her, a behavior that she could not quite figure out and strained to discover. In order to gain time, she tried to shield her face under a meticulously neutral expression: she really needed that job. The edge of the chair—one of those uncomfortable, cheap office chairs—was digging mercilessly into her butt, and she desperately needed to pee. It's just nerves, she kept telling herself, it's just nerves."

Ana lifts up her pen and skeptically observes the tight blue scribble with which she has filled half a page. Too bad I didn't think of bringing the typewriter, it would've been so much faster. Vacation is almost over; she has been cooped up for almost four weeks in this rental apartment, one of those depressing places near the beach, furnished with impersonal plastic stuff. Ana is thinking that the time spent here together with her mother and her son—both at once is simply too much—would have been absolutely unbearable were it not for those long solitary hours spent furiously writing, covering page after page with fragmented episodes from her past. Her watch has stopped, but it must be almost noon; through the ludicrously small balcony that passes for a terrace she can see the bathing suits hanging out to dry in neighboring windows, a sure sign that lunch is close at hand. So it won't be long before Curro comes back from the beach with his grandmother, and Ana wants to make the most of these last few minutes of peace to put some order to her papers, her writings, her letters.

"Dear Ana: I am beginning to suspect that there is a masochistic streak in you. Spending a sweaty month in one of those awful little beach places surrounded by family is nobody's idea of excitement . . ."

The ultimate irony: a letter from José María. They have known each other for many years, yet this is the first time that he has ever written to her, as if suddenly he couldn't bear to be apart for twenty days. She also got a letter from Elena and, coming from her, it was just as surprising:

"Anita dear, I was introduced to your handsome prince yesterday and so, against my natural and well-known aversion to the epistolar genre, I hasten to write to tell you all about it. What better proof of my devotion can there be? OK, OK, I'll get to the point, don't skip ahead, I'm coming right to it. Yesterday was the preview of the *Ultra* series—you know, the one in which my publisher wants to include my cursed book (I'll never finish it, and what's worse, I'm about to finish it, you can imagine the price I'll pay—it'll be a real piece of shit), and I was invited, of course, and so was your Ramses. He was there, hobnobbing with the crème de la crème of the publishing world, very much in his role as "publisher at large," you know, pompous smirk and all. Actually, to be precise, there was only a bit of cream in attendance, since in August not even God stays around in the city, but that capitalistic nerd—my publisher—got into his head the asinine notion that the series should be launched on the anniversary of the publishing company. He's just pathetic, that man. Anyway, where was I? Ah yeah, Dalmau Figueras introduced me to Soto Amón, who was thoroughly charming, the only thing he didn't do was kiss my hand and click his heels in a Hussar salute. Really, Ana, what a fake of a guy, I can't imagine what you see in him. He's as phony as a plastic mannequin, so handsome, such blue eyes, his hair just so, the white silk scarf in place of a tie, yuk . . ."

Letters from José María and from Elena. News from an old hopeless love and about a future hopeless love. Her life is a palindrome. And, on the table, a few crumpled sheets:

"Juan, I guess my letter will come as a surprise. Even though I hate the word, let me begin by saying that this is a business letter . . ." (this won't do, how can Curro be simply business?).

"Juan, after much thought I have decided to write to you. We haven't heard from each other in years, and this would suit me fine if it weren't for Curro. In other words, I am writing because I'm worried about him, because he needs a father to identify with . . ." (awful, awful aggressive beginning).

"Juan, I assume you will be surprised to get this letter. I confess writing it is not easy. I decided to do it for Curro. He is almost five and he needs to know who his father is . . ."

Ana sighs desolately: she is a lot better writing about the past than treading into the future.

His face had a sort of pseudofeminine softness, like the softness of a flabby thigh, his sagging cheeks seemed to tumble down his face.

"We won't be hiring until next year but . . . what'd you say your name was, hon?"

"Ana Antón."

"Antón, Antón . . ." he repeated to himself while he looked distractedly through a list. "Ah, yeah . . . this is very fine. You did well on the tests. Perhaps something could be done, after all." He raised his listless, shifty eyes and looked her over with an air of complicity. "In fact, I'm sure we can take care of this."

She felt the unspoken demand in his words, as if he expected a certain specific behavior from her, a behavior that she could not quite figure out and strained to discover. In order to gain time, she tried to shield her face under a meticulously neutral expression: she really needed that job. The edge of the chair—one of those uncomfortable, cheap office chairs—was digging mercilessly into her butt, and she desperately needed to pee. It's just nerves, she kept telling herself, it's just nerves.

"It won't be easy, needless to say, because there are a lot of people applying for jobs as you know, right?" the under-under-under Secretary of Information and Tourism was saying. His chubby hand, meanwhile, was running up and down the lapels of his coat, a brown and thin armor inside which his damp flesh quivered. The fascist insignia in his buttonhole gave off a small glint.

"You would like to work at the Ministry, isn't that so?"

He smiled a soft, ingratiating smile waiting for her answer, knowing it already, sure of his power. And she had to say yes, she would like it a lot. She wanted to get out of that pathetic institute on Fuencarral Street downtown, with its blown-out neon lights and peeling walls. She wanted to forget about job applications and forms and aptitude tests, about back-stabbing and competition: he was hired because of his connections; she's a shoo-in 'cause her uncle's the vice-president of the bank. Ana took the placement exams at her old high school gym where everything looked worn and dreary. Just a few months ago she had been part of this world, had felt a kinship with her classmates, had shared the common antagonism toward professors. Now, however, the enemy was within . . . in the suspicious looks with which they eyed each other, in the frayed shirtsleeves, in the closed huddles, in the murmurs behind backs. Twelve hundred. There were twelve hundred of them on this cold January day, hating each other and awaiting their turn. They held on to their typewriters greedily and watched each other fearfully, trying to size up the opposition. There were young girls in plaid skirts, prematurely aged thirty-year-old men, fat women sheltered behind their fake pearl necklaces, and a few older men with nicotine-stained teeth. They dragged their portable machines through the halls, avoiding the obstacles, and huffing and puffing in cold fear. In the sidelong glances of the middle-aged men, veterans of many failed attempts, the resentment was clearly visible: What is that young girl doing here? What does she want in this place? These chicks with no family to feed, who wiggle their asses to sway the executives, are stealing my chances. "Most of them are into whoring," said Herme, an acquaintance from the institute, oblivious to the fact that Ana was one of them. He was over forty, had a strawberry birthmark on his forehead, and wore a double-breasted navy blue suit and a scandalous green tie—"Looks are really important in these matters," he proclaimed proudly. He had on white cotton gloves smeared in black at the fingertips, "otherwise my hands get cold," he tried to explain in a hushed voice as if he were revealing a state secret, "and I can't keep up the typing speed required. Neat trick, don't you think?" and he blew on the gloved tips, filthy from so many tries. Ana later found out that he had been eliminated in the first round.

"Yes, of course, I would love to work at the Ministry."

A smile broadened the man's trim, officious mustache; it was a satisfied smile that underscored the proper order of things.

"Of course you would; it's a secure job where a smart girl like you can work her way up quickly . . . particularly being so young. You are very young, isn't that so?"

"I'm seventeen."

“Seventeen, listen to that. If you start at the Ministry now, in ten years you can be at the top. You might even make it to secretary of the Minister himself or something like it. You would like that?”

She would not. Not at all. What a horrifying future, cooped up within official walls, a death sentence measured in steps up the ladder. Nevertheless, one had to say yes, Mr. Under-under-under Secretary, to get that much-needed job.

“Yes, sir.”

“Then, again, your age is also a handicap,” he said lifting the typewritten sheet disdainfully. “Look at all the people who have applied. Older people, people with families, with more responsibilities. People who have been waiting for many months. It might be possible, though, to push you ahead a bit, since you have done so well on the tests and since you speak some French . . . isn’t that right?”

He spoke in unctuous tones, with a sort of oily congeniality that made one feel an accomplice to his unstated indecent proposals. Adolescent Ana, job seeker Ana, Ana Antón, party to unmentionable betrayals. “Most of them are into whoring,” Herme had said while he chewed on the tips of his glove.

“Yes, sir.”

“Oh, don’t call me sir, Anita, aren’t we good friends already?”

It was dizzying. Ana was still much too young and he was powerful and she was dying to pee and he smiled and she felt uncomfortable and guilty and his double chin quivered and Ana realized that her fears were well founded, that he was laying an ambush.

“And we’ll become even better friends,” he cleared his throat, suddenly doubtful, but added quickly, “you’ll need to review your French a bit, don’t you think? Look, I like you. You seem smart and I would like to help you. As you might imagine, I’m a very busy man, but I’d be willing to help you with your French for a few days so that when I recommend you for the position, you will be prepared. So, let’s see, perhaps this afternoon”—he appeared to be checking his appointment calendar—"yes, this afternoon's OK for me. So, if you can manage, we can work on your French."

Her answer shot out automatically, a naive line of defense that she mumbled as she retreated further into her chair:

"In the afternoon I have to go to school."

The man was quiet for a few seconds, his eyes hardened, but he forced another smile:

"Fine, after school then."

"No, no, I can't. I don't get out until very late and then I go home. My parents don't let me go out at night."

"Look here, kid . . ." his voice was strained now and audibly threatening, "this is a very good job we're talking about. It requires a range of qualifications that I'm beginning to think you may not have. I told you that I'm a busy man. Nevertheless, I offered you my help, but you are not cooperating . . ." he started to smile in a last attempt. "You should be friendlier with me, you know."

"I just can't."

Silence. And then, finally:

"All right." His cheeks shook with suppressed rage; he put the candidate list away in a drawer, took another file, opened it and immersed himself in it. Without looking up he added:

"I'm busy, girl, and I've already wasted enough time with you. I doubt that you'll get any job, being so rude. If anything should come up, my secretary will be in touch with you. Good afternoon."

Ana would have liked to say something. She wanted to stand up, icy and self-righteous, and find the precise words to express her contempt, to insult him and not break into tears.

"Didn't you hear me? Why are you still here?"

And weakly, helplessly, she stood up in silence and, in silence, she left.

But if Ana's story were to be told, it would have to begin earlier, before the job search and the institute at Fuencarral Street, before poor

Hermenegildo of the nearly white gloves, before the Ministry full of men with quivering double chins. The whole thing started with the death of the flasher.

Ana Antón must have been around thirteen or fourteen; she was tall and flat-chested, and the boys that gathered at the school doors ignored her in favor of fleshier adolescents; she had still not started menstruating and, in short, felt very sorry for herself. The sophomore year had unleashed a sort of race among the girls. They would arrive with ruddy cheeks for the geography class with Miss Ordóñez, that deaf and shriveled old lady, and they would sit sleepily on the benches, looking out the windows and watching the December morning reluctantly brighten up. A rumor would spread through the rows of seats, "Luisa's got it, she's a woman now," and they would all look at the girl in the front, the focus of the whispers, sitting very straight and hiding her body's secret. Not Ana. The sophomore year came and went, then the junior year, then senior year started. It will never happen, she would think to herself, I'll never be normal, how awful. She ate a lot of bread because she had heard that starch made the tits grow, but she didn't see any results, and month by month she fell behind her friends. At last, one day, she found stains on her panties and, to her dismay, felt dirty and ashamed. Her mother provided her with some crude terry cloth strips—they had to be washed and the blood smelled bittersweet—and told her:

"You can't eat or drink anything cold, no ice cream or anything of the sort, you can't shower or take baths, you can't swim or sit in the sun, you can't wash your hair, you can't run or do sports. And be on the lookout, check your skirt often for blood."

Restraints, restraints, restraints. All those stupid and unnecessary taboos that make you think that "that" is a sickness. And, like so many others at thirty, Ana still finds herself saying "I have the curse," still and at thirty, even though she well knows that it is perfectly fine to shower and to eat ice cream, that it makes no difference if she washes her hair with the tampon string dangling between her thighs.

But we were talking about Ana looking like a rail and not having her period. At that time there was a math professor at the institute, a pale old man with dry, scaly skin. He would set the plumper girls on his knees, those ten- or eleven-year-olds with hints of breasts, mere carnal intimations. "Don Emiliano is so nice," they all agreed because he did not yell, because he hardly ever failed anyone, because he went over the incomprehensible material and did not care if anyone understood, because he would bounce them on his trembling legs and caress them with his coarse, reptile hands. They were so young. One day in the subway, when a well-dressed man stood close to Ana, his throbbing hand in his pocket bumping against her buttocks, her only reaction was surprise. She turned, looked at the man's unruffled face, and moved to the other side of the car. But the train was full, and in a while, what a coincidence, there was the old man again rubbing his baggy trousers against Ana's buttocks in that sweaty, reeking subway. All the way to San Bernardo–Cuatro Caminos, the end of their ride, the old man did not budge. When they got off at their station, she told her friends, did you see that poor man, how his hand shook, it must be that disease, isn't it called Parkinton's or something like that? They get the shakes all over and then they die. It was the first time and she did not know. But she learned. Later she became wise, they all did, to these bloodless daily attacks. They learned about stray hands that pinched, about rubbings on the bus, about the shock of finding something hard—poor babies, still ignorant of erections—against your thigh or your hand. They learned about those passing shadows—fathers of large families, exemplary husbands, hard workers all, no doubt—who lunge at you in the middle of the street, their eyes on fire, whispering unknown brutal words, I'm-gonna-stick-it-in-your-you-know-where, I'm-gonna-fill-you-with, I'll-grab-you-and, and since they didn't know about those things, they would shrivel against the wall, or look away horrified, or hold their breath while the man's own bounced off their bodies. Some-

trouble." That was street-wise Paquita, who lived in the tenements outside Madrid and who, by now, must be married and overwhelmed with kids or, who knows, perhaps she is a prostitute in the inner city.

(Six or seven years ago Ana had gone back to one of those cheap movie theaters, for old times' sake. On that occasion the short, ratty-looking old man with calloused working hands who sat by her side did not touch her; he did not rub her with his leg either. He just stared right at her while he masturbated. It was all very quick. The jacket he had folded on his lap moved rhythmically up-down-up-down propelled by his hidden hand. Then he began to pant slightly and a handkerchief emerged from his pocket and disappeared between his legs. Ana did not feel any kind of surprise or even disgust about this scene, only a sense of guilt often evoked by wretchedness. That lonely and useless ejaculation she interpreted as evidence of a vicious cycle of misery, a dying marriage, a fat, aggressive, unhappy woman, pleasureless sex on weekends and holidays, yelling and resentment at the dinner table, spankings meant for each other but meted out to the children.)

Another time, at the end of her junior year when Ana was fourteen, she remembers wearing her first straight skirt and some high heels borrowed from her mother. School was out already, but all the girls had returned to check their final grades. They were crowded around the bulletin board chatting spiritedly. Some had their hair teased in the latest fashion; others were heavily made up and eager to show the rest how grown up they had become in one week of vacation. Then all hell broke loose. Teodora, the mean janitoress, ran or rather trotted heavily up and down the halls with her flab all awobble. Miss Cardona, the Latin professor, unmarried and virginal at sixty years of age, was screaming wildly as she leaned against the door to her classroom. Father Bernardo patted her hand, trying to console her with rote phrases that resembled litanies. Don Justo, the headmaster, fidgeted about with an air of being the-only-man-who-can-handle-this. The girls would have loved to come near and find out what extraordinary event had caused Cardona's collapse, but Miss Barbara, the old lady with the white bun who taught advanced French, was keeping everyone in line at the end of the hall. "For heaven's sake, don't come near, children, this is terrible, and to have this happen on the last day of the school year." They began to put two and two together when the police came out of the classroom escorting a small man with stiff bangs, round bulging eyes, an overcoat buttoned all the way up in spite of the heat, what a scream, look at his bare legs. His calves were white, bowed and hairy, and his feet tottered inside enormous shoes. As the officers were dragging him out, much too energetically, the little man smiled with a dumb and devilish expression and tried to greet the gallery of girls with a triumphant, if handcuffed, wave. It was not difficult to identify him: it was the same old flasher, the one that had haunted her pubescent years, the one who lurked in the dark corners of the subway. And the rumors spread like wildfire. When Miss Cardona walked into the teacher's lounge he was already there, sitting in the best sofa, erect and satisfied, with a deranged smile, infatuated with his own miserable flesh, with his sagging, wrinkled body, with his decrepit organ which he so delicately rubbed before the scandalized gaze of the teacher. And Ana, when she saw the little man leave, skipping on his pathetic legs, felt disturbed with intimations of her own troubles ahead. When she arrived home, her father broke the news:

"We're broke, you'll have to go to work. What I mean is, no more school. You'll take some business courses in shorthand and accounting and find a job in a bank."

For some strange reason her thoughts turned to the little man, that little man who had filled her young years with fear, to his small, forbidden pink prick that had menaced her for so long, to the splendidly ridiculous finale in which, that very day, he had been arrested and sent to jail.

"What are you doing, mommy?"

Curro, slinking up with cat steps, is touching her knee. He stands on

Nine

"Some awesome summer, man," says Zorro, using a toothpick to clean his nails. He has painted them alternately with red and green polish, and his hands look like multicolored paws. "Every one's on the fast track, I don't know what it's all about but I can sense it, I can smell it, man, I can smell it. It's freaking me out."

These are crazy times. There are schizoid winds blowing in the endless hot summer nights, each so unique and yet identical in the sheer scramble for survival.

"Gimme me a drink, man, don't be so damn cheap."

"Forget it, pal. Pay your tab and then we'll talk."

They start their rounds early, as the first shadows fall. Every night they put on their warpaint and make ready for battle, hoping at least to lay claim to the same spot as the night before. The once bustling neighborhood has been taken over this summer; it loses its character and identity in the dark. As if on exodus from a remote city, from daylight, from another life, they converge on this microcosm and mingle with locals like the old anarchist, loaded as usual, spewing booze and bits of lung as he wheezes and hacks in your ear. He is fighting the same old battles: "Sombitchin' bastards, think they're hot shit, where the fuckin' assholes been when we was in the trenches?" He will sleep it off on an outdoor bench and take advantage of the steamy night air.

No one fails to show up at the unestablished time and place—lords and lackeys, veterans and rookies, heroes and groupies.

"Hey you ol' queen, you wanna drink?"

"So, the Bard is calling you his ol' queen this early. He must be shitfaced already."

"Don't be too sure. You know he can handle his booze."

They begin their ritualistic rounds while the sidewalks shimmer in the heat of the fallen summer sun, in those first hours of the seemingly eternal night. First they survey the scene, sniff each other out with nostrils eager for the exotic aroma of the dark. They light their first joints of black hashish, which usher in their authentic existence, and swap the obligatory greetings and passwords of their caste.

"You're looking good, Zorro, decked out like Ali Baba himself."

"Just wait till you see the forty thieves. My entourage is just around the corner."

The laughter—friendly and lethal at the same time—serves to mark one's territory and to establish turf, turf that will be defended if the lines of demarcation are crossed.

"I hear you just got back from India."

"That's right."

The first stop is always around the outdoor tables in the square, where they review their troops and plan their nightly maneuvers. They wash down their thirst and perk up fading highs with the cheapest beer on tap; they launch their initial blind attacks, enlist new recruits, and draw up hasty battle plans.

"Who's that jerk with the red scarf around his neck?"

"That's Teresa's latest, the Italian she's been bragging about for the last three weeks, another one of her wimps."

“And the blond chick over there, the one with the shapely ass?”

“That’s the kid that hitchhiked down from Oviedo, she’s Marga’s friend and not a day over sixteen.”

“No wonder she’s so hot.”

“Look, there’s Cuervo scoping her out right now, just look at him hover, he might even buy her a beer. The cheapskate would do anything to get his rocks off.”

“Hey, listen, is it true that someone here has seen Olga?”

“Yeah, the fat broad that looks like a walking bazaar, the one that’s sitting over there next to Músculo.”

Later on, if there is some nice new flesh, or even if it is not so nice or so new but just available, the sights are set, the object is focused, the gun is cocked, and the hunt is on.

“I hear you just got back from India?”

“You heard right. Are you the one they call ‘the Fox’?”

“Yeah, I’m Zorro. Did you run into Olga while you were there?”

“I saw her, three weeks ago in Goa.”

“Let me get you a beer, and you can tell me about it.”

Zorro moves easily through the crowd staring at his long mane, his muscular body, and the flashy satin threads he throws on every night. He always looks as if he’s wearing everything he owns, but each morning he seems to find a new treasure chest filled with yet more tunics and embroidered vests and low-slung bell-bottom pants that show the hair below his navel.

“You’re cruisin’ for a bruisin’ decked out like that. One day you’ll get your face bashed in, Zorro.”

“No way. Folks step aside when they see these biceps. What d’ya think I lift weights for, girl? To protect myself from whatever can lunge at me from the cover of night.”

The muscles of his arms ripple with tattoos like the fox with a silver snout that he had etched in blood to remind him of who he wanted to be, the Night Fox, and make him forget who he had been, Antonio

Abril, the attorney who disappeared one day, disguised in satins and flowing hair, flipped out on acid and cheap booze.

(Amid the chaos of that infernal and endless August when dates, names, and memories become confused, Zorro can still take time out to remember when he last ran into Ana, Olga's friend. He had just gotten out of bed, so it must have been late, and he was still sober, too sober he had to admit, at least sober enough to meet the 3:00 P.M. train and to pick up Mustafa—a.k.a. Pepe from Huelva, who was bringing in a score of first-class hashish. Anyway, there was Zorro, causing a scandal or just giving a thrill to the bored crowd of waiting passengers, dressed in an Indian tunic with open flaps, tanned and naked as a jaybird underneath, waiting for the train when he bumped into Ana, with her bratty kid on one side and her mother on the other.

"What're you doing here?"

"I'm off on vacation."

"How touching, you, your mom, and your kid. I bet you're going to one of those family resorts," Zorro commented sourly. "The very thought warms the cockles of my heart."

Ana blushed and stammered something like "well, that's how it is," avoiding his glance. Since they had nothing better to do while waiting, they decided to get some coffee at the bar. Ana asked him about his wrist and told him that she had seen him slash it.

"Were you among the screamers or the fainters?"

"Neither," Ana answered with growing irritation. "I could give a damn if you slit your throat."

They were silent for a moment, not knowing what else to say to each other. Finally Ana spoke:

"Have you heard from Olga?"

"No. Not for quite a while." Zorro's expression clouded.

"The last time she wrote me was at least a year and a half ago," Ana continued. "I'd like to know how she's doing. I think about her a lot."

“I bet you do,” Zorro replied sarcastically, “looking back longingly on your wild years, now that you’ve settled down, huh?”

“Why are you always attacking me?”

“I dunno, guess I’m a naughty boy,” Zorro shot her one of his dazzling smiles.

“More like a pain in the ass, Zorro. Lay off me, will you? I don’t feel like getting into it with you.”

Zorro burst out laughing, “Fine, fine, let’s call a truce. Know what? There’s someone around who just saw Olga in India. If I hear anything, I’ll let you know.”

“Try to get me her address.”

Their chance meeting conjured up in Zorro all the painful memories of the Olga that he had lost.)

The first hours are for reconnoitering, before embarking on the long journey that ends up being the short and well-worn path connecting, like an umbilical chord, five or six grungy and crowded dives that reek of semen, narcotics, blood, and vomit. A few will not show up at the first haunt, and their absence will be noted: “Where’s Marga tonight? I wonder who she’s latched on to. And how ’bout the Governor? He must be on another one of his head trips, holed up in his room and bouncing off the walls.” A few leave and others take their places, seeking out one another as if they were returning to the safety of the womb, searching for the warmth and protection of their kind, the misfits and dropouts of this ragtag band of rejects and rebels. “It’s the revolution, man, no way ’round it.”

Zorro is tottering on the last edge of lucidity while doing his best to get as respectably loaded as possible on one long drink. “That’s what it is. Know what I mean? We’re revolting with our painted eyes and long beards, we’re insulting in our drunkenness, my very presence, our very presence, is unbearable because we’re free, because we do what we feel like, because we’re dirty, we’re destructive, we’re poor and proud of it.

It's the revolution, my man, that's all there is to it. We're like cancer." The carcinogenic Zorro is leaning against the bar at Toño's, a rundown place with mangy, stuffed bulls' heads hanging on its filthy tile walls. He is haranguing Trompeta, the broken-down trumpet player, and his patient drinking buddy, Barítono.

"Listen, sir," Trompeta tries not to slur his words, "I don't recall ever being introduced to you."

"Sure you have, Trompeta. You saw me yesterday, the day before, and a couple months ago. Come off it."

"No, sir, I do not know you. And you do not know me. We have never met, you do not know who I am, you have no idea who you are talking to."

"All right, Trompeta, all right. Let's say I don't. Tell me, c'mon, it'll only be the hundredth time."

Trompeta leans on Barítono in an admirable attempt to keep from falling over. Barítono turns his sensitive nose away from the stench that engulfs him and distractedly cleans his fingernails with a broken matchstick.

"Here, just look here. This is me. But I bet you still don't know who you're talking to."

Once again out come the old IDs, the union cards affirming that Manuel Aguirre Blanco, the trumpet player, belongs to the musicians' guild. It is only one typed line that the drunkard reads over and over in a nostalgic voice while he points to the document with his fingerless stump, what remains of his left hand after a freak accident cost him his once musical fingers.

A few leave and others return to take their place in this endless turnstile, where each entrance and exit is noticed, commented upon, and recorded in the annals of oral history. It is impossible to escape so many eyes, so many snake eyes spying on themselves in an eternal serpentine chain that bites its own tail. It is easy to tell who is sleeping with whom, how often and when, by tracing the wake of trichomoniasis, gonorrhea, crabs, and other venereal diseases that serve as their common bond. The germs spread as rapidly from one to the other as from cell to cell in the same body.

"Hey, d'ya hear? There's trichomoniasis going around. I'm gonna get myself some antibiotics just in case."

"Who brought it this time?"

"Tina. She caught it in Ibiza."

"Shit. I slept with her last night."

"Well, now you know, you've got it on your prick. So get away from me—those bugs just might decide to play leapfrog. Didn't that bitch warn you?"

A few leave and others return, and still others lose themselves along the path to enlightenment, as the mystically inclined Buddha would say. Olga finally left on her much trumpeted quest, one that she dreaded as much as desired.

"I still remember when we saw her off at the north train station," Patitas recalls, scratching an old scab caused by his braces on legs crippled by polio. "She was so scared looking at us from inside that train, leaving all her friends behind and going alone on her adventure. She looked terrible in those bib overalls she'd bought for the trip, and was scared stiff, just petrified." Patitas had found the right expression. "With those big eyes of hers filled with tears, she was too petrified to even say goodbye. Don't you remember?"

First she took the train to Barcelona, then the cargo ship to Turkey, then trains, buses, who knows what all, until she arrived in India, the eternal India of nirvana and freedom.

"I've had it, Ana. The bastards I work with exploit me, harass me, hate me because I'm not one of them, because they sense I have a wild night life, because I don't wear a bra, because I'm alive. I'm leaving. I'm getting out of this shit hole and never coming back."

So Olga, the secretary in spite of herself, tied to a salary that barely made ends meet but still able to scrimp with admirable asceticism, made good her promise and disappeared one afternoon in search of their communal dream.

"Hey, where in the hell has Mito been hiding? It's been a while since I've seen him pushing his stuff at the Rastro flea market."

"Fuck, Zorro, haven't you heard?"

"Heard what?"

"About Mito. He's as good as dead. The pigs unloaded a full can of tear gas right into his face at a demonstration. He's finished, a vegetable, brain dead. His heart still beats but that's about it. For all practical purposes he's gone, but the doctors still have him hooked up to machines . . ."

"Goddamn . . . but Mito was never into politics."

"So what? Maybe he got caught in a crossfire, nobody knows for sure what happened. It took us a while to even find out, because the papers gave his real name and no one knew who in the hell this Guillermo Fernández or López, or whatever, was."

Some never return. The wall on one street corner, where a young Marxist was gunned down by a fascist death squad, is spray-painted blood red every night. Every day the wall is whitewashed, and every night it is repainted to pay homage to the boy who also thought he was part of the revolution. He nurtured it with blood as red as the clandestine painting in his honor.

For the first few months, Olga wrote regularly to her mother, to her friends, and to her beloved Zorro, with whom she had maintained a self-destructive relationship that she could neither submit to nor reject. As time passed, her letters became so infrequent that the miles separating them seemed multiplied in a chasm of silence. Except for erratic penstrokes with news from someone someplace who happened to run into her, all trace of Olga was swallowed up in an oriental mist that allowed only brief glimpses. She left a painful vacuum at first, but by now their memory of her had all but vanished.

The walls of the women's restroom at Panas are splattered with refined obscenities and subversive graffiti, erotic sketches, and urgent calls for help. As you squat about a foot above the doubtlessly syphilitic toilet seat, you can gratify both your aesthetic and your physical needs by reading the graphic messages while peeing. Huge red letters crisscross the grimy corroded door: "Release Torcido Now!" "Carmen Luvs Torcido." Below, in a pinched black scrawl, "M" adds her own sequel: "Torcido loves only me, but don't let that stop you." Mora is absorbed in her reading, trying to make sense of the words and to keep from keeling over. She is high as a kite, and her head reels with smoke, fog, emptiness. Her panties are bunched around her ankles, and her tiny floral skirt is damp with semen. A bitter and salty smell seeps from her groin as she hovers between revulsion and abject misery: "God, I'm so fucked up, I'm so stoned."

Zorro was detached: "Yeah, I've seen her around, at Panas, Galáctica, Toño's, all over. But we'd never exchanged word one till last night."

"Hey, you're getting to be a real Henry Miller, Zorro darling. Maybe you should write a story about it? It's just the kind of sordid plot that turns you on. Admit it, it makes you feel like a real hunk."

"Who, me? I'm no macho. You know I've got a feminine streak. Besides, she fucked me. She was thoroughly plastered and stunk like the plague, and I was pretty shitfaced myself. It all happened in a flash. I was just making my way to the back of Panas, and all of a sudden she grabbed my hand and pulled me into the women's room and fucked me. There you have it."

"Amazing. It must've been uncomfortable as hell. D'ya do it standing up or on the floor?"

"Standing up, you idiot, you know how tiny those stalls are. Standing up and flushing the john every few minutes to stifle the noise."

"It must've been a quickie, huh?"

"Well, you know, it was pretty exciting. A couple ins-and-outs is all it took."

Nuria, the Catalan woman who went to India with Olga, had returned to the clan a few months before. Her news was already skimpy, painful, and stale: "Olga was gettin' weird, you know what I mean, really strung out. India can be a pretty heavy trip, so heavy that some don't make it back. They get stuck and never snap out. You understand? They never snap out of it. India can tear you apart, it can snarf you up if you don't know what you're looking for. I'm no moralist, you know that by now. Or picky when it comes to drugs. I've pumped myself full of anything. As far as I'm concerned, no orifice need be spared. But—how can I say it—there's always something that tells you to turn around, to look inside. Or else you just lose it. Fuck, Ana, I've seen so many lose it. You get to the point, I dunno, you get to the point where you just don't give a damn, not for anyone or anything. You'd rob your best friend if you had half a chance. That's how Olga was the last time I saw her. She was heading into the void, a zombie, and hanging out with real slime—this Dutch couple, both of 'em junkies, who had some kinda hold on her. I'd guess it was heroin. She never said so, but I think when I left her in Nepal she was into needles."

They were well into the night and scores of glasses had been emptied when Roberto went for Músculo's jaw and cracked it open: "You fuckin' sonofabitch, you shitfaced cocksucker, you damn pusher, I'm gonna tear you apart . . ." Barítono shed his habitual cold shell and stepped in between to save Músculo from Roberto's mad and powerful rage. He had to acknowledge that Músculo formed part of their clan; he had to step in. Blood was thicker than water and the gang had to defend itself against outsiders. Músculo was spitting out teeth, stumbling, bleeding like a stuck pig. That was when Roberto pulled out a gun, and everyone froze in their tracks.

"Stash that iron, and leave on the next breeze, man. No one's lookin' for trouble." Of course it was Zorro who had taken charge. Who else? With all eyes focused on him, he was the shepherd of this nocturnal flock.

"I'll kill 'im, he's a two-bit sonuvafuckin' pusher. I swear I'll kill him."

Roberto had just been released from a psychiatric ward. He had a long history of electric shock therapy and other socially acceptable tortures. He drifted in and out of the unemployment office just long enough to pick up part-time jobs unloading freight—that is, whenever he could, whenever he felt like it, or whenever there were enough burlap sacks to heave onto his powerful frame and rip oozing gashes in his massive shoulders.

"I'll kill him, I'll kill him." Roberto was sounding less convinced. Someone shoved a drink under his face. It was Reina, the owner of the bar: "Here, it's on the house. Drink up and start walkin'."

"Cool it, dude," Zorro cut in, adeptly giving a friendly tone to his cool yet stern words. "I don't know what you've got against Músculo, but it's not worth it. Look, you've already ripped his mouth open. That's enough, man, you're even—no matter what your grudge. Now split."

Zorro's hand gripped his ebony cane just in case things came to blows. But in the end Roberto acquiesced and put away his gun. He was more than eager to leave and disappear into the anonymous night rather than force a showdown. He was surrounded—Zorro directly in front, Barítono to one side, Barón, Turco, Pedro, and Lanas casually positioned to flank. They were ready to defend the clan, their only reason for being, the last stronghold of their existence.

"So Músculo finally got his face bashed in. Roberto's off his rocker and strong as a bull. Now this poor bastard has his jaw stitched up in wire so it doesn't fall off. He'll have to wear that metal brace for a couple of months at least."

"But why would Roberto want to kill him?"

"How do I know? Sure, the word was out he was pushin'. OK, Músculo deals, but he deals to friends. And he's not into the heavy shit."

Yes, Músculo deals. It is common knowledge. But he sells to friends, just to make some bread. He is the local score and rarely does hard stuff. He is not into the big traffic or part of the cartels. Sure, he pushes hash or a little opium, if it is on hand. Heroin or morphine? Hard to tell. If he does push horse, it has already been cut and recut ten times over. But he is no kingpin, nor is he hooked on it. Sure, he'll sell grass or hashish and take his slice off the top, but he sells at a fair price to his buddies. He's a good guy, Músculo, that softy with the big brown eyes and long limp hair. He has a certain shy way about him, and his decimated build makes his muscular forearm seem even more powerful, that single chiseled forearm with bulging veins that earned him the nickname of Músculo, that unbelievable forearm which, as rumor has it, he developed by jacking off.

The back tables at Toño's are occupied by the old guard, the longtime regulars who have been pushed to the wall by the advance of the younger, louder, and stronger newcomers. Seated in stoic silence on rickety chairs at decrepit tables, these ancient night riders refuse to relinquish their ruinous lives. Their three-score bodies are emaciated by alcohol and crowned with bulbous noses traversed with broken veins. Seated under the mangy bulls' heads with chipped horns, they seem like just so many more trophies of a past era, and piteously mistreated trophies at that. They were the beatniks and nonconformists of their day; they lived on the fringes of society, never married or reared a family, never ran in the rat race. Men like the old gypsy who cracked his voice belting out flamenco tunes, and the would-be bullfighter who still dresses the part with a broad-brimmed hat to cover his broken dreams. Or the poet, the artist, the ladies' man, and the amateur matador. Together they form a nostalgic homage to the past, drink their last dregs to the good old days when the women were there for the asking, and console one another with cheap wine that stains their glasses and their toothless smiles. Even though their once firm skin now sags in wrinkled folds, they proudly state that they were forged in bronze and recall their whoring nights with higher-class prostitutes than proper officials could ever boast, or the show girls they would wait for at the stage door exuding the aroma of the finest wines. Their wrinkled hands can no longer remember the softness of the women's shoulders, nor their pubic down, nor the vaporous feathers of their tinted boas. They formed the fringes of the society of their era, but this bronze race neither understands nor admits the new counterculture. A chasm exists between the frayed but proud lapels of the old guard and the Indian tunics of the young. Toño's might as well be partitioned, with one half reserved for the silent and long-suffering veterans and the other half taken over by the boisterous and aggressive newcomers. These closed and self-contained marginal cultures repel each other.

"So tell me, how was Olga the last time you saw her? What'd she have to say? It was in Goa, right?"

"That's right, in Goa, at some friend's place. I barely spoke to her, but I don't think I have good news to report."

"Goddamn, go ahead and spill it."

"OK. Just cool it, will you? Don't get so uptight. I didn't even recognize her at first."

"But how could you, had you ever met her before?"

"Yeah, in Barcelona, where she caught the boat, before she left. She spent a couple of days at Miguel's, and I was living with him at the time. So we got to talking. I told her that I hoped to get to India within a year, that kinda stuff."

"Can you get on with it?"

"Where was I? Yeah. I hardly recognized her at first. She was like real thin, haggard, kinda old. I'm not sure how to describe her to you. Her eyes were sunken, and with huge dark circles around them. She was wearing heavy makeup to cover them—eye shadow, kohl, the works. Poor kid, she looked really wasted."

"D'ya talk to her?"

"Sure I did. Well, like I said, we were at a friend's place. There must have been fifteen of us and we were all pretty stoned. Some were sleeping it off, others were eating or just talking. It started to get dark, so someone lit a few candles. I hardly knew anyone, just the couple that owned the place and maybe one or two others. She was right in front of me, just sitting there all by herself and rolling her head from side to side. There was something familiar about her face, something really familiar, even though I was pretty gone myself. It had been a beautiful day, real sunny, and the sun set over some spectacular orange groves on the far shore. I'd done some acid that morning and was really trippin', it was fantastic, I tell you, and I was feeling great. All of a sudden I started obsessing on Olga. Something told me I knew her, so I picked up one of the candles and went over to her. That's when it came to me. I put the candle up to her and looked her full in the face. I knelt down beside her and said, "Olga, Olga. Damn, it's good to see you! Don't you remember me? I'm Sol, from Barcelona. Remember I told you I'd be coming. Well, I made it."

"And what'd she do?"

"Not a thing. She stopped rolling her head back and forth, she looked up and just stared at me. I was still tripping, maybe that was it. Zorro, you know how a little sugar cube can make you really see into people. Well, all of a sudden, I freaked out. All that iridescent makeup she had on started flashing in the candlelight, and at first she seemed dazzling and magical. But then suddenly . . . I dunno, suddenly her face started disintegrating right in front of my eyes. Her flashy makeup turned into a mask, I don't know how to explain it, as if it was just a hoax, and behind it I could see Olga's face. It was, like, suspended in the air, and as solemn as . . . as a skull. I dunno, Zorro, but she really spooked me, staring at me out of those dark sunken eyes of hers. They were like bottomless pits and I was afraid I'd fall in. There was something terrible there, the way she just looked at me with that ghastly expression. Finally, she said something in English like: 'I don't know you. Who are you? You've got the wrong person. I don't know who you are.' That's pretty much what she said, and in this slow, almost cruel, voice."

"So what'd you do?"

"Nothin'. She really had me freaked, so I backed away, just pushed myself back without even getting up, without taking my eyes off her, until I found one of my friends and told him how panicked I was. He took care of me, and she just stayed in her corner, babbling I don't know what all in English."

"Are you sure it was her?"

"Positive. When I woke up the next morning, I looked for her, but she was gone. I asked my friends and they told me that, yes, she was a Spanish woman named Olga and that she'd been around for quite a few months, mostly with a Dutch couple, but that they'd left without her. She'd stayed polluted ever since and was completely busted, with no place to live and surviving on handouts."

"And into needles, right?"

"Afraid so, Zorro. I think she was using needles, at least that's what they said. Here, I can give you the address of my friends in Goa, and maybe you can locate her through them."

This sure is a crazy summer, overcharged with diseased sperm and paranoia—a stifling summer. In the dark, one can almost hear the missing call for help. Their cries are more like appeals to a new realm, to a different dimension, to the unknown, to destruction and death. It is a summer when everything is up for grabs, so no one is shocked by the news about the Governor. He has fallen victim to the insanity of the long summer nights.

"Fuck, man, what a mess, that guy's always been a jerk . . . and now this." Barítono's words are cold and calculated to shield his horror with cynical bar talk.

"What's up, what's happenin'?" Cuervo has just walked in, as ready as ever to catch up on the latest gossip.

“Nothin’ . . . just that the Governor went’n did himself in.”

“Jesus H. Christ . . . how?”

“That moron. You know he hadn’t stepped out of his place for a

 week. He was having another one of his panic attacks and was just too paranoid to show his face outside his four walls.”

“So . . . ? What happened?”

“So nothin’. So last night he jumped out his window. But the jerk didn’t figure that it was only the third floor. He must have smashed his nose, maybe broken a bone or two, what do I know, he got pretty bloody. So what does he do? He drags himself over to the elevator and gets onto the roof, but now it’s more like the sixth floor, and jumps again! He’s squash now, man, better believe it.”

“What a fuckin’ jerk. Hey, how d’you know he jumped twice?”

“Because Marga was there. She’d gone over to get him out of his cave. You know she is, or was, crazy about him. Well, it seems he tried to make it with her and couldn’t get it up.”

“So what else is new? That’s par for him.”

“Anyhow, Marga falls asleep and wakes up in the middle of the night with this feeling, kinda like a premonition, and she sees him standing buck naked on the windowsill. Suddenly it occurs to her what’s goin’ on, she tries to get up, but she’s too late to stop him. He’s already jumped. So Marga looks out the window and she sees him spread out like a frog on the patio tiles. She races down the stairs without a stitch of clothes on, and when she gets there, he’s gone and there’s only a bloodstain. Meantime, it seems he’s in the elevator on his way to the roof. So while she’s down there, screaming like a banshee and waking up the neighbors, who by now have got their windows open, what happens? Here comes the Governor soaring down from the roof, and he splatters like a watermelon right at her feet.”

“Yech! What a bummer!”

“What a fuck-up.”

“Some jerk.”

“Damn worthless bum.”

"Such an ass, a bloody asshole."

A black shadow of death and paranoia hangs over them, a shadow of grief and bone-chilling anguish. It had been ten days since the Governor last dragged his six-foot mortal frame over to Panas. They had gone like inseparable blood brothers to a disco called the Blue and White, where they plopped down at the tables to shake off their drunkenness. That was when Torcido's thugs walked in, pulled out switchblades, and started slashing up some blond kid who was dancing in the corner. The kid was from the slums and hollered, bleeding, to his friends: "Bros, help, they're stickin' it to me." But his "bros" either were nowhere around, or did not hear him over the music of Stevie Wonder that no one bothered to turn off, or were too afraid to come to his aid. No one did, and he just squirmed in the midst of the multicolor strobe lights on the dance floor, grimacing in pain and fear. After Torcido's gang forced their way at knifepoint into the street, they ran into the Baron, drunk as a skunk and harmless as a fly, on his way to meet up with his friends at the disco. Until that night, Torcido had stayed clear of the enemy clan even though he hated them; but that night, with fresh blood on his hands, he felt the surge of power. When he saw that the Baron was alone, he started slapping and insulting him: "You faggot, you bloody queen, you queer, step aside. You're in my space." That is when the Baron's clan of friends rushed out. Under the orange glare of the neon lights, Zorro bashed Torcido over the head with his ebony cane, and the Governor slashed one thug's back with a broken bottle. Even Barítono managed to knock someone down before he got his head split open by a chair and had to be stitched up in an emergency room by a nurse who had seen it all before and pretended to believe that he had run into a doorjamb. All the lights in the neighborhood were switched on, and from above they could hear the shouts: "Drug addicts, murderers, bastards! We're calling the police!" Yet these respectable citizens barely dared to look out the window, smug and comfortable as they were in their secure condominiums.

"Zorro, Marisa's looking for you."

The members of the clan do not understand solitude, or cannot abide it, and seek safety in numbers. They are there every night, cultivating their poisonous and stormy brotherhood. The Baron, Barítono, and

Patitas are crammed close together, apparently deriving some comfort from the warm sweat exuding from their thighs. There is Pulga, all doped up and talking wildly. Next to her is Julita, her cheeks flecked with paper stars, tiny stars that only exaggerate the bewildered look on her face. Patitas has already singled her out as a novice. He sits down next to her, making sure that his leg brace rubs against her trembling thigh, and proceeds rhythmically and conscientiously to feel her up. Julita is horrified and about to lose her nerve when Pulga intervenes: "Bug off, Patitas. Just leave my friend alone." Someone decides to crash a nearby swimming pool for a night dip.

"Zorro, I'm talking to you. Here's Marisa, she's been looking for you."

"Yuk."

Zorro seeks himself out in mirrors, and when there are none at hand, he must search for his reflection in any and all of his night companions in a self-conscious attempt to keep a grip on his image. Whether it is by his satin clothes reflected in a darkened store window, or his tattooed fox, or the multiple pierced studs in his earlobe, or the ravaged faces of his clan, Zorro reaffirms himself and kicks a little more dirt on the grave of the lawyer Antonio Abril whom he fears above all else. Zorro holds court in the pub like an emperor on a throne, favored with tenderly seductive glances from his women, "Zorro darling, let's get together," and there's a lot of feather ruffling until he decides on his choice for the evening.

"You're hyenas, always laughing it up about how I make it with all the chicks. But there you are, ready to pounce on what I leave behind. I get the bad name, I do the dirty work, and then you come along to gorge on the leftovers. You're scavengers, just like crows."

Cuervo gloats slyly, thinking that Zorro's words are dedicated to him. He is flattered. Then Zorro remembers Olga and feels a hollow silence in the midst of the noise—a craving in his stomach for what never was. Wrapped up in his image of the roaming Night Fox, he could never commit to Olga. He was young then, and he confused commitment with the traditional clichés. For him, freedom meant having no ties that bind, so he kept running away from Olga. For all the years they knew each other and for all they went through together, he never once gave her the key to his inner self. He regrets it now.

"Look, Zorro, you old fox. Here comes Marisa again, just begging for your favors."

The Bard is a few yards behind them, with one elbow on the bar and using his free and expert hand to grab ass onto Lanas, who smiles, not knowing what else to do. Lanas is obviously upset, but he is still a kid, barely eighteen, and just starting out on this tortuous night path. A few months back, he pierced his ear and proudly wears the delicate gold earring under the wooly blond curls that earned him his nickname. The Bard understands the vulnerability of apprentices to the cult of vice and tries to capitalize on it. With deft fingers he fondles Lanas's firm buttocks and latches onto his balls. He is hurting Lanas, who tries to look as if he could give a damn but whose eyelashes flutter with fear. "Hey you, you young cock-tease, let me buy you a drink and give you a little feel-up, huh? I won't hurt you, you little slut, you're ready for it, you're ripe. If you're still a virgin in body and soul, no sweat. I can show you the best time, and I won't even charge you for it."

"There's the Bard trying to suck dick."

"Wishful thinking . . ."

There is no doubt that the Bard is the veteran of the gay scene, the longest-reigning queen of the night. Though now past fifty, he still faithfully cruises the bars. Rumor has it that as a young man he smoked opium, sniffed coke, and was into heroin. Now he is gaunt and burned out. His intense eyes glower relentlessly like coals from under his white eyebrows. They say that he used to be a college professor, that he taught something heavy and brainy like history or philosophy until he got fired on charges of moral turpitude. They caught him after class one long-forgotten night, widening the horizons and the anal canal of one of his students. They say that the boy was crazy about him, but he was still convicted of seducing a minor and served a number of years in prison, even though those in the know said the kid was already a long-time pro and expert in the arts. No matter what they say, the fact is that after his release the Bard never went back to college teaching. He used his new-found freedom for decadent games and kept a lot of bars in business along the way. The Bard, the unrivaled patron of our daily and nightly sins.

"Turco! Man, it's been years. What mean tricks have kept you in hiding?"

"Me? Nothing new. I've been doing a lot of thinking lately."

"My God, Turco's been thinking. Now that's news."

(Let him alone. It's not worth the trouble to talk to him. He's an absolute basket case. This wild summer we've been living has fried the last few neurons he had left. So now Turco is pursuing the hunt and capture of young chicks. He wants to find the total woman who will wash his underwear, pamper him, and do his cooking. The fool says he feels old and worn out.)

"Life is tough, you know. I'm fed up with being broke, never having a dime to my name, being fucked up all day long, wasting my time."

"Ah ha. So now, at thirty-seven, you're just coming to realize it?"

(He has even stopped smoking hash. Turco says he wants to climb out of his hole. He is the walking parable of the prodigal son who finally gets his head on straight, raises a family, and turns into the conventional holier-than-thou man of the house. Yuk, it's disgusting.)

"Come off it, Turco. I saw you just the other day on Princesa Street, trying to make it with some real hot chick."

"You're a retard, Zorro. She's an average kinda girl, kinda pretty, kinda young . . ."

"And a cock-tease. I bet you haven't scored with her. I bet she's got a rich daddy who can set you up in his business."

"I'm into other things now, Zorro, things you'd know nothing about."

Patitas has gone over to the next table and is into his usual harangues—praising the magnetic force of the pyramid, mocking Carlos Castañeda, revving himself up on his own mysterious powers. Patitas is in his mystical phase—he thinks he is going to get it on that way, the poor guy. With his useless legs all wired up, he resorts to magic to attract women. Patitas unfolds his most persuasive charms before Marisa, who bites her nails, hardly listening to him while looking lustfully at Zorro, so close at hand yet unreachable.

"Look, Marisa, now is the time to transcend the body, to go beyond the old stale rituals. What are you doing here tonight? You're looking for a lie, for the crumbs of an affection that doesn't exist. If you don't rid your karma of that suffering, you'll never attain perfection and ecstasy." Patitas then joins his hands together and rolls his eyes back in an expression of rapture.

Zorro is slowly but enthusiastically moving in on Ainhoa, who is going to take some doing. Ainhoa is a beautiful, enigmatic, magical, and fearsome woman, a Basque woman physically and emotionally scarred for life by torture.

"Hello, Zorro, what's up?"

"Hi, Marisa. See for yourself, just hanging out with the crowd."

"Me too. I was supposed to meet a friend, he was going to give me some . . ." Marisa is getting caught up in her usual nervous litany of excuses and boring explanations, which Zorro does not even pretend to hear, ". . . and so, sure, I had to drop by, even though I didn't think he'd show up, you know how it is . . ."

"Mmmhmm."

"Er, um, I had something to tell you . . . but I forgot."

"Well, just make sure you tell me if it comes to you. It couldn't have been too important if it slipped your mind."

"I guess not . . . well, I was wondering . . . what're you doing tonight?"

Misery loves company. The clan is hanging on to every one of Marisa's words, greedily lapping up her embarrassment, her submission, and her shame. Each one is cynically calculating the ripest moment to sink his teeth into her, and each one feels touched by the glory reflected off the great Zorro. Every female's sniveling invitation to the chief is seen as an open invitation should he reject her. Ah, the communal glories of the clan.

"Well, I guess I'll be heading home. I have things to do."

"Oh. Yeah . . . me too. I only mentioned it because—now I remember what I wanted to tell you—because a friend asked if I could score some hash for him, and I heard you've got some great Afghanistan. He was wondering, would you come with me and meet him at Galáctica and let him try some?"

"I did have some, but I'm all out. If I hear about any, I'll let you know, Marisa."

Zorro kisses her deeply, introducing his warm expert tongue between her teeth. Even though he is not the least bit interested tonight, he does not want to put her off completely and would rather take a rain check just in case. One never knows.

"Wait, Marisa, if you're going to Galáctica, I'll go with you. OK?" Amparo, her blond hair carefully braided, jumps up ready to lend a friendly shoulder to cry on, ready also to ensnare Marisa into her delicate lesbian web, woven with perhaps a compulsive yet tender love.

"What a slut you are, Amparo. Are you leaving with her?"

"Yes, I am, Zorro. And look who's talking! You're the biggest whore around."

Ainhoa had spent long months in a solitude crammed full of people.

When she was released from prison during the amnesty, there was something irretrievably broken in her life, in her sense of place, in the once fiery beliefs that had led her to Basque militancy, to commitment, and to torture: "You whore, you filthy bitch! Who are your contacts? Let's have some names." She was subjected to nonstop mental and physical torture for two, three, four days. The days and nights blurred in that police dungeon where she left bits of body and soul. She spent the following years in prison as if in a deep freeze, and the sun of freedom would never again burn brightly enough to take the chill from her bones. She filled her nights with teeming bars to escape the too familiar panic, the void. The hollow shell, all that is left of the once tough Ainhoa, is now disillusioned, fear-ridden, and alone. No one has managed to get close to her in these last few months, almost no one has even been able to have a coherent conversation with her, few have seen her pale mouth break out of its frozen grimace into a smile, and no one has caressed her abused breasts in this, her second life. Then, step by step, the stealthy Zorro started patiently closing the circle around her, and tonight there is something erotic in the air. Tonight Ainhoa finally allows herself to lean her head against his strong and sweaty body, she huddles against him, gradually shedding her defensive outer layer. Zorro feels a hot rush in his stomach, and something akin to tenderness—a long-forgotten sensation—creeps through the shoulder where Ainhoa, now brought back to life, sears him with her feverish desire. There is a hush, and the clan falls away from them as if separated by a layer of thick summer fog. From far off they can hear the Baron talking about his new job, two striptease acts in a new gay club, and out of the mist reverberates the high-pitched voice of Peca, who was recently released from a mental institution: "I'm so afraid they'll send me back that when I start to feel a little weird, I take the pills myself." The last time she was committed was when she stripped off all her clothes in a classy boutique and tried to fuck the salesman. Poor Peca, a broken and plucked little bird. But all of them and all their voices seem distant. Zorro, with the warm weight of Ainhoa in his arms, senses that something strange is about to happen this evening at the zenith of summer's heat.

Torcido's gang has come in, and as usual, everyone keeps a respectful and cold distance. They are thugs and savages, those dregs, survivors of years of malnutrition, with their discolored teeth, their flashy black leather jackets and mirrored sunglasses. They silently taunt with their hands in their pockets caressing their switchblades: "You bastards, you pretty boys playing it cool, all decked out in your ratty threads, you're not worth a piss, you damn fags." Torcido sucks on his broken tooth and spits loudly through the crack to draw attention to himself: the great Torcido, the source of the best shit, the underworld kingpin—even though he is no more than an expendable middleman for the heroin cartel. He is in a party mood tonight, celebrating his release from jail for carrying an unregistered handgun. It was all they could get him on, even though he already has a few murders to his credit and a lot more knifings. Just six months ago he cut up a kid for not paying the few bucks he owed. It was a question of principle, of discipline. In the darkness of night you don't dare show any weakness. Just one snitch, just one bad move, and you've had it. In the darkness of night you always have to show who is boss, who is in control of life and death, just to stay alive. Torcido now owns a Kawasaki 750, drinks scotch, and spreads fear because fear is a form of respect. Torcido tells himself that fear is the basis of his success; it paved his way out of the slums, where he left behind a father who had never officially recognized him, two sisters—one a cheap whore and another who ekes out a living cleaning toilets—and an older brother, a motorcycle stuntman at local fairs, who is killing himself just to make a living. In the abject solitude of his own private hell, Torcido feels both his triumph and his squalor on the cold tip of his knife.

It is getting light outside, and through the window Zorro can see the stifling gray dawn rise over the asphalt. On a night just like this he had come to his senses after scraping bottom. It was in San Francisco after a month of tripping on acid—thirty doses in thirty days—a frightening trip into the void. It was on a night like this that he tried to escape California and his own schizophrenia on a tramp steamer to India, that ruthless India where he searched for Olga relentlessly. It was on a night like this, in Afghanistan, that a mutual friend handed him a ripped-out page from a notebook where Olga had scribbled that she never wanted to see him again. It was on a night like this that Zorro caught a plane back home, with India and all the utopias of his dreams up in smoke.

"Because once you've been to India, man, what's left? It's the end of the world. There's no other place to escape to and no more remote paradises to seek. When you've gone to India, man, you've hit rock bottom, of the world and of yourself."

It is getting light outside, and the accumulated heat of the entire summer is rising up like tar fumes from the pavement. Behind him, the muffled sound of cloth lets Zorro know that Ainhoa is getting dressed, licking her wounds like a wet cat. An occasional glimmer of tears threatens to cloud Zorro's vision as he thinks of her—the broken, barely alive Ainhoa, whom he was unable to love and at one point had almost raped when she scratched him with her fingernails in a moment of terror and desperation. It is getting light, and the sky hides behind grimy clouds. Ainhoa silently closes the door behind her, disappearing for good. Zorro wearily lets his eyes fall on a scrap of paper lying on the table. It is Olga's address in Goa, an address that Zorro knows has no use. The choices were made and the game decided long ago. There, outside the window, he sees people like Ana, people who begin their workday at the break of dawn, a time that for him marks the end of so many things. Zorro slowly rips up the piece of paper while the clouds open, hesitantly at first, and then break into a fierce storm—like the deluge of judgment day, like the end of the world. It is an early sign of winter, and from high above, the scent of January descends. Summer is dissolving into the first rites of fall. This has certainly been a wild summer, an insane summer, a summer of tense fears and lonely anxieties—the ultimate summer, the rock bottom of summer.

to swallow the soup in a huge, dark dining room full of tables occupied by just one person. What do you think of that?" "Awful," mutters Ana. "You at least have Curro, you're not all alone . . ." There we go again with the same story. Ana herself is positive that Curro will leave when he's fifteen, sixteen, seventeen at the most; it's the natural thing to do. He will be little consolation if any in that future of senile loneliness. At times, in spite of the restrictions that having this child impose on her life, in spite of the pleasure of seeing him grow and turn into a more mature, more independent, more complex being day by day, Ana secretly wishes she could keep him small, still in need of her help. There is no doubt—mothering temporarily cushions the pain of loneliness, covers it up.

"You were really lucky to have gone to a nonreligious institute rather than to a nun's school," Pulga is saying.

"I guess so," answers Ana. Now it seems that she lucked out on everything, on having a child, on attending that place with crumbling walls. Perhaps so, perhaps she was indeed lucky.

"You have no idea what it is to be around nuns. Just imagine that I never once masturbated until eight years ago or so . . ."

"Seriously . . . that's not possible."

"It is, it is," insists Pulga. "I had no inkling of things like that. And besides, we'd been so corseted with all the stuff about sin, hell, purity, the Virgin Mary, immoral acts . . . I wasn't even all that clear about what an immoral act was supposed to be. I figured it was something like having your heart race while watching Troy Donahue films, just think of it . . ."

And that's what she was like when she got married, Ana realizes. And that's what I was like on my wedding night, thinks Pulga. There is a momentary lull in the conversation as each gets lost in her own web of past frustrations.

"Chrissie, will you please finish eating that once and for all without any more spills."

It is a taut, impatient voice. At a nearby table a man in his mid-thirties chews absentmindedly, surrounded by children of varying ages, three boys and a girl. They don't speak and hardly even look at one another. The kids sit stiffly upright on their chairs and stare at their food, one nervously banging his shoe against the leg of the table. "Look at him," whispers Elena, "there's your typical separated father." The city is full of them on weekends, desolate men dragging behind them an intimidated group of children—through restaurants, zoos, movies, circuses. The men are pushing forty; they married at a time when marriage was still thought to be forever, and now with tears and anguish have unmade their established lives. Every Sunday at the same time they pick up their kids, feigning happiness, and together they kill some hours that are uncomfortable for all. They bring dolls and trains for the small ones, ask the older ones about school, and the afternoons drag on amid monosyllables and embarrassed silences, each a stranger to the others.

"So, by the way, did you hear about Julita?" Elena pipes up suddenly, her voice unusually cheerful.

"No, what about her . . .?"

"Ohhhhhh, a lot happened while you were gone. She's having an affair."

"No kidding," answers Ana, remembering Julita's tearstained face during those early stages of her separation.

"Yep. What happened was that she had to be at work by nine, and since the publishing house is so far, every morning at eight she would pass the Legazpi intersection in her beat-up little bug . . ." Pulga starts one of those exhaustively detailed explanations for which she has such a weakness.

"In short," Elena cuts in, "she's sleeping with the traffic cop that works Legazpi."

"Who?"

"What I said, the traffic cop."

"Is that for real? What a scream . . ." Ana laughs.

"I mean it. What's more, he's apparently a young guy around twenty-five, bearded and handsome to boot.

"I've seen him and he's really cute," Pulga adds. "I drove by there one morning just to have a look at him."

"She says he'd been winking at her and cracking jokes whenever she stopped at the light. At such an hour and in such a traffic jam it must be quite a tickle to run into someone like that . . ."

"But how'd they get together?"

"Oh, simple. One day she hit the red light and he said he'd like to have lunch, that he was on the morning shift, and asked if she would come by and get him at three. And Julita went, and . . . so it goes. They see each other every day, I tell you, this is real passion."

"That's something."

The restaurant has run out of coffee, so they leave and wander about a bit through streets that already smell of autumn. "Let's go over to Mercedes and Tomás's pub," Elena suggests. "Nahhh, it's always so jammed . . ." "Not at this time. C'mon."

Galáctica is indeed just about empty, almost sleepy itself at siesta time. Sitting at one of the tables Mercedes sips slowly from a tall glass filled with crushed ice and crème de menthe. Next to her is her son, his face half hidden behind blond, curly hair. "Hi, Lanas, long time no see." He gets up to greet them and turns on the charm. "What would you like?" he asks, doing his friendly host bit. "Three iced coffees." "Some liqueur or anything else?" "No, no thank you." And he moves toward the bar dancing inside his cowboy boots and wiggling his tight ass.

"So, how's it going?"

Ana takes advantage of the boy's absence and leans over to Mercedes with a questioning look.

"Bah," she shrugs her shoulders with irritation, "horrible, as usual, we were just having an argument, I just don't know . . ."

She's tanned and beautiful, her well-rounded arms jingling with

Moroccan bracelets. And her nails—the only thing that recalls the old Mercedes, those nails, long and almond shaped, painstakingly polished in bright red.

"I don't know how I do it," Mercedes sighs and throws her head back melodramatically. "When I was twenty and slim, I dressed like a forty-year-old lady. Now that I'm forty and generously endowed, I wear feathers, ruffles, and shiny stuff like a girl half my age. When I was fifteen I would slip off my socks at the bottom of the stairs and change into stockings. Now I have exchanged the panty hose for funky anklets. When I was a child, parents wallowed in respect, and kids would get slapped for the smallest thing. Now that I'm a mother, my children completely ignore me, and I'm the one that has to chase after them and treat them with infinite caution. And as if all this wasn't plenty, I discovered sex only two years ago. My God, any minute I'm going to have to come to the conclusion that my whole life has been a mistake."

Tomás is forty-two, Mercedes forty. Lanas just turned eighteen, and their daughter must be over twenty. A while back, not too long ago, Mercedes and Tomás were a young, happy, terribly ordinary couple. He was a well-paid executive at an import-export firm. She had a flower shop—a kept woman's trade, she would say—a small operation that ran on a deficit. Their children grew up fast, much too fast. The girl went on the pill at fifteen, and the boy dropped out of school at sixteen. By the time he turned seventeen the whole family smoked pot: you had to help them through the changes, be a pal to your kids, erase the distances between you and them. Tomás resigned from his position, Mercedes sold the shop, and they opened a bar for the young crowd: music, strobe lights, a long-haired and kinky clientele. A new occupation to stay close to the children, their own watering hole to keep tabs on their long nights away from home. Mercedes darkened her eyes with kohl, lightened her hair with henna, and exchanged her Dior perfume for sticky patchouli. Tomás hung up his tie and donned faded jeans ("You go to any length trying to understand them," he would say plaintively, "but they don't appreciate it at all, let alone lift a finger to get close to you. And meanwhile, like an idiot, you are wearing jeans that skin you alive instead of the looser pants that you really like, jeans that squeeze your balls and rub you raw"), and one day he even shocked the clients by showing up with his hair tightly permed, the Afro-style curls hovering over his distracted young father's face. And under the protection of his frizzed hair he feigned being an old connoisseur as he talked about coke and sugar cubes, about shooting up, about the merits of a brownie.

"I don't understand them," Mercedes is saying as she follows her son's maneuvers out of the corner of her eye, "I don't understand them and I don't know what else to do; I feel overwhelmed."

Mercedes and Tomás are ready to understand and encourage their children's every whim. "But imagine," they exclaim with stupor written all over their faces, "they just don't want anything." They are the golden offspring of the upper classes; they have had all they ever wanted, never known family problems; they are privileged in a way that doesn't even arouse their interest. Tomás and Mercedes's children pierce their ears with multiple gold wires (he) or have a rose that turns into a snake tattooed on the nipple (she), and their total turnoff includes money. They need only a few loose coins to pass the nights cruising the urban underworld, through each and every ghetto hangout except that of their parents. Today's adolescents, Ana figures, came into the world either too soon or too late, and their lives are so messed up that they have turned old before their time. This whole scene is radically different from her own teens. It is barely a decade ago, but that other world seems rusty, ancient history.

Ana was around eighteen when she finally landed a job in a bank. Those fortunate few who got in at the same time showed their glee: "It's a secure position, now all we have to do is wait for the regular raises and promotions." For the rest of your life. Ana shivered at the very thought, at seeing herself in her co-workers, particularly in those who were past their first youth and who were condemned to feel old-maidish already just because they were not yet married. Or those others, the mature women who rushed home at lunchtime to fix their husbands' meals, "thank God the children eat in school." Or Antonia. Antonia was short, chubby, rounded, with not one angle to her. She was maybe twenty-five, wore gobs of makeup, gold-plated necklaces and bracelets, always a feminine touch as she had been taught. Her coquetry was the shop-window kind, adorned with cheap paper ribbons as if she were shy about offering the merchandise. Sometimes, during one of those midmorning lulls in activity when the men in the department leafed through a newspaper or discussed the Sunday soccer match, Antonia would polish her nails in fiery provocative reds. It was very likely her only transgression, the only escapade of an otherwise proper middle-class girl who always wore her skirts discreetly at the knee, the hose carefully taut and without runs, the collars primly buttoned up above abundant breasts that were themselves conveniently bound by a stiff brassiere to prevent the possibility of inviting movements of the flesh. But there must have been more erotic adventures inside her vapidly innocent head, Ana seems to remember, because one day Antonia showed her a package that she was cautiously hiding in her purse:

"Here, come and see what I got."

Ana looked. It was two pairs of diminutive black lace panties, two dark, fluffy clouds.

"Oh, some underpants . . ."

"Panties, panties, don't be so crude," interrupted Antonia, blushing. Antonia had a peculiar and rather sick prudishness about the most mundane things.

"Very pretty," Ana said, somewhat at a loss for words.

"Yes, aren't they?" Antonia replied. And after a pause she added in an almost naughty tone, "I like only black undies, you know? They're more . . . more feminine."

On Sundays Antonia and Blanquita, the tall, thirtyish girl from the international department, the outdoorsy one who always wore pants (all this love of nature and open spaces inevitably smacked of Christian youth outings), and also Lola, the teller, a big, good-looking Andalusian who was the liveliest of the three, would call one another up before the unavoidable family lunch.

"What do we do today?" they would ask and ponder.

"Oh, I don't know," one would answer. "We could try Danilo, or go to Gladys for an ice cream, or . . ."

"The other day I went by Galatea and it looked very animated, there were lots of guys . . ." another one would venture.

"Well, Antonia suggested going to the outdoor cafés on Rosales Boulevard. She wants to check out the guy with the mustache that she likes, see if he's there."

They would meet at Lola's to finish primping. Lola was the leader, the one who set the pace. They would arrive at four-thirty or five. They would crowd around the bathroom mirror, pass the mascara around, add mysterious touches of shadow to each other's eyes, mauve strokes or dabs of blue at the edges, and then eyeliner. They would discuss clothes, try out things that they had chosen the day before ("what're you gonna wear?" they had inquired previously), and get the others' opinions . . .

"Does this jacket go with this skirt?"

"You look great."

"Really?"

Finally, close to six, they would go out ready for battle, giggling arm in arm down the streets, drunk with eagerness for life, bumping laughingly into other pedestrians, flirting naively with anyone who crossed their path. After a few false starts—there was not much room for selection—they would head for the jammed quarters of some new cafeteria to have some cream puffs, or hot dogs at Galatea perhaps, or to one of the sidewalk cafés on Princesa or Rosales for rum and Coke, which they slurped feeling very grown up. They would spend the afternoon eyeing the guys who flittered about and whose sexual desires were much more defined than the vague sentimental dreams of Antonia, Blanquita, or Lola. Sometimes, when they felt particularly daring, they would go barhopping in the evening and follow a time-honored itinerary: spicy potatoes at Samuel's, a glass of wine in Moncloa in one of those bars packed with men who gaze calculatingly as if saying, "No, not those, they're the kind who want a serious relationship." Occasionally, with slight trepidation, they accepted a round from a stray husband in his forties who was not quite sure which kind they were. They accepted his invitation and then left, suddenly puritanical, like modern-day Cinderellas scurrying home before midnight, leaving the would-be Romeos with the frustration of having paid for a nonprofit round of drinks. And they would part at the entrance to the subway or at the bus stop, and each would arrive home in time for a late snack, with her Sunday clothes a bit crumpled, and then do the dishes in the dimly lit kitchen. Later, languidly undressing in a room still full of stuffed toys—moth-eaten mementos of childhood—they found their uncertainty and anguish surfacing once more. Sadness about another week of work ahead of them, disenchantment about those black panties, so hopelessly feminine, that Antonia would take off all alone in her grotesquely pink and childish room, with subconscious awareness of her failure.

Ana wonders now whether they are still doing that sort of thing, if Antonia, Blanquita, and Lola continue to keep the same old ritual of cream puffs. Or whether, on the other hand, they have come to realize the absurdity of it all and are now embittered about lost time. Like all those other women between thirty and forty who know themselves to be losers, those who understand that they have missed the boat, all those intelligent, sensitive, warm women who have given up on life because the changes came too late for them, because they feel inadequate. Like Amanda, that woman from Catalonia who worked at the bank, who was married with children, and who, when Ana got pregnant, advised her to stay single. "Don't get married, Anita, don't do it. I have wasted my life but you are young and times are so different now, don't marry." That morning Manola, the vice-president's secretary, was also at the impromptu gathering in front of the newly installed coffee machine:

"Sex is a bloody pain," she declared, "and that's all men ever think about. I have four children already and if I could, believe me, I would sign a contract right now to be forever exempt from it. Pepe is a real maniac, I can't even stand in front of the sink without him coming from behind and grabbing me. It's always a struggle to get loose, 'Hey, let go of me, I'm busy, water's getting all over the floor, let go . . .' He's always cocked."

"If you ask me . . ." Amanda pondered thoughtfully, "I wouldn't mind Ferrán doing that sometimes, wouldn't mind it at all . . ."

"Oh, c'mon, it's awful . . . they climb on top of you and wham, wham, wham, it's all so easy for them," Manola laughed, a bit surprised at her own obscenity, "and you, in the meantime, worrying about getting pregnant. Imagine how *that* would grab me now that Mari Nieves is already seven."

The second round of coffee is finished, Lanas has asked his mother for money and has left, people are beginning to stream into Galáctica, and Mercedes has had to take up her position at the bar. Ana has been dutifully informed about Cecilio's latest: he's gotten into sending personal ads to the *Leisure Guide*, the kind that read "GWM, intelligent, sensitive, cultured, seeks lasting friendship and contacts of every type." Elena has railed against the essay she has finally managed to finish . . . "real crap, I mean it, you'll see." They have discussed their possible preferences in the upcoming elections, talked about Kafka's letters to Felice, about the Basque country, about the end-of-the-summer sales. They are about to say their goodbyes when Elena blurts out, looking at Pulga with biting eyes, "But you still don't know the best part . . ." "Well, what is it?" Ana wants to hear. "Ask her." Pulga reddens, smiles, hedges, lights a cigarette. "Hey, can somebody tell me about this? C'mon, what's going on?"

"Simple," says Pulga. "Do you remember that hitchhiker we picked up one day coming back from the pool?"

"No."

"Yeah, sure you do. The circus acrobat who was so terribly exotic . . ."

"Ah, yeah, he was very young and from England or something, right?"

"That one, he's American. Well . . ."

"Well, what? I'm beginning to fear . . ." says Ana with a smile.

"Ah ha, the worst," Elena interrupts. "She's already taken him on, seduced him, has him living with her, the works."

"Damn, Pulga, you're something else."

Pulga angrily chews on the filter of her cigarette. Why does everyone seem to demand an explanation from her? Why does she have to justify herself, anyway? Elena is looking at her with a sort of superior smile, and Ana grins benevolently. "OK, I'll admit that I worry sometimes about this habit of making it with ever younger guys. What do you think, that I'm oblivious to it or what?" Pulga volunteers. "I know that I need someone my age and that Steve is only nineteen and that he barely speaks any Spanish and that we have nothing in common: he doesn't read, doesn't like movies . . . it's a mistake but I really like him a lot. What can I do, he's affectionate, fun, he wants me, and I need him."

"But you must be bored stiff with him."

"It's not bad at all. You see, we sleep rather late. While I work, he rehearses. Then we eat together, I work some more, and he goes off to the circus . . . I meet him there, watch the show and . . . well, you just can't imagine what that is like. Each night, when I see him with his glittering outfit and walking the tightrope I fall in love again. Didn't you ever, as little kids, fall in love with a flying trapeze artist? That's what it's like, he dazzles me every time. And I do love him, I love him because he is affectionate, naive, tender . . . I know it won't last forever but in the meantime . . ."

They all laugh, and while the laughter still lingers in the air, Ana begins to feel depressed. It may well be true, after all, that Pulga's relationship is far more real than hers. Ana feels incapable of passing judgment on her friend's delirious affairs because she is afraid that, in spite of everything, they are much more convincing than her own, easily more authentic than her infatuation with Soto Amón. More so than those long years of misencounters with José María, whom she loved so much and with whom she shared so little. Even more than living with Juan and sharing everything, hatred included. Ana somberly realizes that she has wasted half her life inventing nonexistent loves and that this Soto Amón of her thirties is nothing more than her latest, most sophisticated artifice.

Eleven

Candela has not been sleeping well lately and feels very tired. This morning they all woke up late, and in the rush—the kids would never make it to school in time—she inadvertently mixed coffee and chocolate in all three cups and did not realize it until, still groggy, they had a sip of the brew. There was no milk either, so they ended up going out for breakfast at a nearby cafeteria. The children, who cherish this sort of domestic misadventure, especially when it means being late to school, were delighted. Candela then ran to her office to find Mrs. Matas and her autistic ten-year-old son already waiting. The child stares blankly into space; he sits motionless, unreachable, a stranger even to himself. Candela sighs: her own children are beautiful, intelligent, healthy. What a joy. Jara is five years old, Daniel just turned nine. Before she knows it they'll be independent. It is funny how close Daniel's birth seems to her, the time when the boy was merely a diminutive bundle, all blotchy and still. At the time she was not at all sure she wanted a baby. But she went ahead and had it. With Jara there was no doubt, she was wished for and sought after. Two years before, Daniel's father had jumped out of a window. Candela had not taken him seriously because he regularly threatened suicide, rolling his eyes wildly about, or feigned insanity attacks, throwing dishes around and bashing his head against the wall. That day he opened the balcony door with a melodramatic gesture. "I'm gonna jump," he said. Candela did not pay much attention, go right ahead. He straddled the railing. "Candela, did you hear me, I'm gonna jump." It was truly a polished and disturbing performance, considering how high up he was, but he had done it so often that Candela—noticing how tightly he clung to the railing—would not indulge him. "Hey, don't be silly, c'mon, get off. If you don't watch it, you're gonna fall over one of these days." The next minute she looked up and he was not there. It was all so very quick, he did not even scream. From the balcony Candela saw him down on the sidewalk, a broken body in an unlikely posture. He must have fallen over or fainted, she thought, I'm sure he did not mean to jump.

Jara's, though, was a much-wanted pregnancy. And a difficult one. It was difficult to give birth alone, once again, in a hospital full of couples. No one came to see the baby girl; no man paced outside while she was in the birthing room. It had been the same with Daniel, but Candela was very young then. With Jara she was older, she had accumulated years of loneliness and exhaustion, and she resented the repeat performance. With Jara, too, she had to face up to people's strange reactions. It seems that our pseudoliberal society accepts the existence of an unwed mother of one child. But if the single woman insists on her disorderly ways, if she blindly dares to have more children by different fathers and attempts to remain alone, then, ah, then it becomes thoroughly unacceptable. "That poor Candela," they begin to murmur, "what a mess of a life." And they turn up their delicate noses in disapproval.

In any case, Jara is Vicente's daughter. On the surface he is an economist with Marxist leanings. In reality he is a conventional man dulled by his fears. He never for a moment forgot that he was married and had two children, and he made sure that Candela did not either. (One day Vicente asked her if she believed in God. He was cheerfully shouting from behind the shower curtain, it was two in the morning and time to erase the traces of their adulterous love. "No," Candela answered. "What? Not even a little bit?" he insisted playfully. "You must believe at least a little bit." "No." "All right, anyway, please try to think of your childhood faith"—he showed a comically desperate and dripping face—"and pray to your favorite saint that my wife is not awake and demands to make love, augh, I couldn't stand it . . ." Candela managed a grimace at the joke, but she noticed the bitter taste inside. Bitterness at the reminder of their precarious bond; bitterness, too, for the other woman, his legal wife whom he humiliated with those words. Suddenly she felt their sisterhood, their kinship in gender and suffering.) The marriage was going on ten years and Vicente had assumed his role as orthodox husband, affairs included.

In the beginning the relationship with Vicente had been perfectly under control. Candela was a strong woman, a competent and decisive adult. She led a full life that revolved around her work and her son. It was she who did the chasing, and Vicente was both charmed and shaken. "What captivates me about you," he once said, "is that you are an original who demands unique responses." They had very little time together because he had an idiotically busy schedule; whenever they saw each other it was always at Candela's place. He would call when he could steal a few hours, she would say yes, he would arrive, they would chat for an hour, make love during the next, smoke a cigarette. Then he got dressed and left. At other times, for the sake of variety, they would make love first and then smoke and talk during the next hour. Their first meetings were sheer joy; they sniffed around trying to get to know each other, and everything was a joke. But little by little Candela began to feel anxious. At first she tried to share her problems with him, tell him about her life, her thoughts. Vicente would look at her distractedly, floating above their conversations, obviously bored.

In time Candela learned to bring up only those topics that interested him. And this meant himself or their relationship. Soon their ritual became etched in stone: he called, she said yes, he came over, they made love, smoked and talked about Vicente (or vice versa), he got dressed and left. It became progressively harder for Candela to swallow all the waiting around, the unfulfilled desire to be with him and have him be part of her world, the unspoken words, the simple wish to walk cozily down the street with him, hand in hand. She disguised her frustrations behind smiles and unwittingly began to alter her life to accommodate him. First she started staying home in case he called, later she would do nothing but wait for the moments they could spend together. Until one day he said: "You know, Candela, you appear to be quite unique but actually that's not true. You're an absolutely conventional woman." Candela was hurt and knew that he was right, that she had taken to acting the part of warrior's rest. The fact was that he led the way, set the limits of their encounters, and then demanded not only serenity, not only patience and understanding, but also surprises aplenty—and very little, if anything, now distinguished her from the submissive, unhealthy, alienating role of his legal wife. Once Candela ran into her at a party. She was still young and good-looking, yet there was something aged and unattractive about her. Perhaps it was her mouth. It was hardened, a mouth scarred by saying "no" too many times. Or her affected hairdo, obviously from an expensive stylist. Her designer clothes were an unhappy compromise between fashion and tradition, too much gold jewelry adorned her. She was a rigid, unreal person, a caricature almost. But her eyes were human and alive with sadness, they cried out for help in spite of herself; from behind the grate of her lashes—thickened with too much mascara—the frightened prisoner inside peered out. Candela did not wish to look into those eyes because they hurt.

Those times were turbulent and painful in other ways, too. Candela was working in the outpatient clinic of a gigantic, orthodox, and murderous psychiatric hospital. The clinic was the recent invention of a

was saying some very sad things from the pages of *The Notebooks of Malte Laurids Brigge*; he spoke of death, of terrors, of insanity, of inward absences. By late afternoon she felt feverish. The sun was set-

ting in the window that framed the mountain peaks, filling the room with shadows and Candela's head with ghosts. In a corner of the room, next to the engraving of wild horses in full gallop under the moon, her mother's image appeared suddenly, smiling at her with her full aging face. "Candela, honey," she said gently, "there is something very funny that happens to women, I mean, it's happened to me often enough," and she mimicked her words with her stubby finger, gathering them in a clump. "There's this woman who takes a dirty handkerchief, fills a bucket with hot water, and pours in some detergent. She soaks the handkerchief for a long time. Then she empties the dirty water, fills it again, and rubs the handkerchief with clean soap. She exchanges the water once more and now adds a bit of bleach to whiten the fabric. Then she moves it to a bucket with a drop of bluing so it will glow, and some softener to make it nice to the touch. She rinses it, wrings it out, and hangs it in the sun so that it will be immaculate. When it is dry she takes it down, sets up the iron, moistens it slightly so that all the wrinkles will come out. She folds it meticulously and puts it in the linen closet, near the sachets so that it will smell fresh. And there is the handkerchief, clean, fragrant, folded . . . then her husband arrives from work, kisses his wife distractedly, goes to the closet, reaches for the handkerchief, snffff, noisily blows his nose, and throws it into the dirty clothes hamper. Isn't it hilarious?" Her mother laughed heartily, swaying back and forth, while Candela did not know whether to laugh or cry, so oppressed was she by this huge dusk that threatened to crush her. Antonia then sat down at the edge of the bed and proceeded to reflect with obvious effort. Candela could hear her thoughts. "My marriage has been a happy one. Almost forty years together, since I married at twenty, virginal and childish. Everything happened very fast, the end of the war, Miguel's return, the courtship, the wedding, quitting my new job as a secretary, the first child, you, Candela. Then the hard times started and I had to watch every penny, spend untold energy in inventing each dinner trying to come up with cheap, interesting menus. The first ten years I cried a little at night, secretly, or in the mornings alone at home, sitting on a half-made bed. Later I got used to it. Got used to burning away the days, waiting for nightfall, being overwhelmed with exhaustion and boredom. You know, I spent so many years without leaving the house—except for shopping and a Saturday movie with your father—that at some point I felt incapable of facing the outside world. I would get lost in the maze of buses, subways, unfamiliar streets. I was even afraid to go downtown by myself. You are so dumb, your father would say when he noticed my helplessness. And in fact I was growing dumber, more lost by the day. One morning, suddenly, I realized that I was almost sixty years old and I had no memories of my life. Only four years ago, after reading one of your younger sister's sex manuals, I finally had an orgasm. Now that all of you are grown, I have a lot of time on my hands. Time to think, to feel old, to know my own inadequacy." At that moment Candela's father materialized, hanging on the coat rack by the collar of his shirt. A little man with a trim mustache, a seasoned minor bureaucrat, a lover of order and hierarchy always opposed to automatic promotions. He was flailing his extremities wildly, not able to reach the floor with his short legs. "Look at him," her mother said, "he's the living image of the good man, committed and right-wing. Do you know that I have always been faithful to him, that I have never known any other?" Antonia was bent over with laughter, hugging her sides as she added, "What useless, silly, morbid fidelity." Candela noticed to her horror that the stump of Margarita's tongue was in her mother's open mouth and that through her laughter she sputtered clots of purplish blood.

She turned on the light. It was eleven o'clock in the morning. Vicente had not come, he had not called. Next to her, on the bed, was the Rilke book that she had read in one sitting, its pages showing no folds that would have indicated pauses. She had a headache and felt drained. She got up and looked at herself in the mirror. The days in the mountains and a slight fever gave her cheeks a reddish glow. Her hair, lovingly washed the previous day, fell thick and shining on her shoulders. She found herself very beautiful and this saddened her. She was thirty years old, in the prime of her life. She sensed that she would never again be as beautiful, with a beauty that was being banally wasted in this cold, lonely hotel room. She was flooded with desire to live, to learn, to know, to try other ways, to work again—perhaps that low-income practice in one of the outlying areas that she had been offered would pan out. She felt the painful urge to reach an adult serenity without resentments, a serenity in the face of loneliness and death. A few months later she got pregnant with Jara, and once it had been confirmed, she broke up with Vicente.

There's a knock on the door and it is Ana with Curro. "I hope Jara's around because this monster didn't want to come and I promised him that she'd be here, you know he's a bit smitten." Curro looks at both of them with unrepressed anger. "Yes, go ahead, take him back to her room."

Jara is a few months older than Curro and he is very vulnerable to her blond, curly charm. She is a real beauty, this child. As Candela says:

"I can't stand it. Why is she so beautiful and I'm not? Why is she golden and curly and I'm stuck with dark, straight hair? In five years I'll have my phone disconnected altogether."

"Why?"

"Because I won't be able to handle it when all the calls are for my daughter," Candela concludes, laughing proudly.

They hear the squeals of the children yelling and arguing. "Where's Daniel?" "He went to the movies with some friends. He's old enough to do his own thing by now." "I can hardly wait," sighs Ana wearily. She wants to talk to Candela once more about Curro's fatherless condition. "I'm thinking of writing to Juan," she begins . . . "and getting lost in all the possibilities," Candela finishes. At that moment Elena arrives, exuberant and talkative as ever, and the conversation is cut short. "What're you two going to get me for my birthday? It's November 15, that means next Saturday," she blurts out. "You sound as if getting older was a real treat," replies Ana. "Well, I figure there's no fighting it, so you might as well enjoy it," giggles Elena.

From the hallway the invisible voices of the kids reach them: "You don't have a little tail, you don't have one," says Curro, obviously showing his. "But when I grow up I'll have breasts and you won't," Jara pipes up in her little voice, "and besides, I'll be able to have a baby in my belly and you won't."

They all laugh at the childish argument.

"Listen to that, castration complex indeed," Ana points out with affection.

"If poor Freud raised his head, I'm sure he'd be so distressed that he'd get hepatitis . . ."

"Nah, I'm positive that he was aware of it . . ." Candela cuts in.

"Of what?"

"I'm convinced that Freud cooked up all this castration bunk to cover up men's inferiority complex at not being able to give birth. Doesn't it bug you?"

Elena agrees. Yes, giving birth is a privilege. Or at least she is beginning to think so. Funny thing, for years she rebelled at the possibility of having a child. All that foolishness about maternal instinct, bah, nothing but cultural hogwash. Now, however, approaching thirty, she is beginning to see matters differently. It's not that she wants a child. No, she has not the least desire to be a mother. But now, and this is the new aspect, she has started to consider pregnancy as a real and individual option. Perhaps it is all due to the fact that for a long time she confused the liberation of women with disdain for them. Liberation was merely a mimicking of the stronger sex, the one in the position of power. One had to adopt masculine values, copy men, repudiate female identity.

Just recently Elena has discovered in herself the pride of being able to give birth, if she so chooses. She no longer considers motherhood a form of servitude. She has finally found herself in her own sex.

Pulga and her tightrope-walker, that simple boy beautiful as a buck, have joined them. She shows him off with unselfconscious vanity, her eyes caress his lithe body, she solicitously pours him a drink, she fusses over him, pampers him. How strange that Pulga, an otherwise intelligent woman, an active, competent woman, should turn into the stereotypical female around her lovers. She acts like an erotically satisfied cat, and Ana cannot help feeling slightly nauseated by it.

Candela puts on some water for tea. In the meantime Elena goes out for some pastries: cream puffs for Pulga's sweet tooth, rolls and danishes for the rest of them. In a moment the table is set and they are gathered around it. Candela brings the whistling tea kettle and a tray with cheese and butter from the kitchen.

"Ugh, Praft cheese . . . no way, I'm not touching that stuff," blurts out Elena.

"Why not?"

"It's incredible, you have no idea of the shit that we consume. The other day I was talking with a colleague from the faculty of Veterinary Medicine and he told me some awful things."

"OK, let's hear it, what's wrong with Praft cheese?" Pulga insists apprehensively.

"It burns."

"What do you mean by that?"

"Apparently they put a match to it during some tests and it caught on fire. Can you believe it, a cheese that burns? It seems that the Praft conglomerate also owns a chain of lubricants, heavy industrial oils and that kind of stuff. I guess some of it must have gone into the cheese."

"How awful . . ."

"Disgusting . . ."

"That's gross . . ."

And they all observe the cheeses with suspicion and loathing.

Elena goes on, "You can't begin to guess the things that my friend told me. For example, do you know that pigs die of stress?"

"Of stress? How come?"

"They have heart attacks. Pigs used to be covered with a thick coat of fat, but since pork fat is not profitable they have bred a new kind of pig that has, instead, a lot more meat made up of muscle mass. Also, they are fattened in a few months, not in the two years it used to take under natural conditions. To do that, they have to keep them practically immobilized in these enormous hangars where three or four hundred animals are crammed back to back and can't move about. And they puff up, get bloated and meaty. In any case, they develop much more meat than their heart, meant for a smaller specimen with some fat and a healthy amount of exercise, can handle. As soon as they take a few steps, zap, they flop over dead."

"That's outrageous."

"Yeah, every time they pack the pigs up to take them to the slaughterhouse, a bunch die just from the effort of getting into the trucks. They just collapse . . . and that's not all. My friend worked as a vet before he started teaching and he visited one of those farms. He says he walked into the barn, slammed the door inadvertently, and killed twenty or thirty pigs instantly. You have to tiptoe in total silence, because if you startle them, their delicate hearts can just stop. Well, you can imagine what the owner thought of my friend's visit . . ."

Their laughter now is tinged with horror, filled with vertigo. "I've no idea how we cope with all this," Candela comments, "our society is absolutely insane." Ana adds her share of good news: hot dogs induce aggressive behavior, beer causes cancer, the jelly around canned ham is made of plastic. Pulga tells of Julita's experience, finding a glob of paper and glue in a can of milk that she used for her kids' breakfast: "Julita may be shy and insecure, but when it comes to defending her children she can turn into a raging fury."

"Yeah, she has balls," Ana concludes.

"Ovaries, Ana, ovaries," Candela corrects her.

"How's that?"

"It's time we stopped using 'balls' when we mean something terrific and 'bitch' to signal something awful. From now on I plan to reverse it and always say 'ovaries' and 'bally' instead."

The giggles end abruptly when they catch Elena's expression. She has just hung up the phone and is now standing there looking pale and distressed.

"What's the matter?"

"That was Javier . . . it's cancer. Javier's got cancer."

Twelve

"You're gonna die if you don't start eating, you're gonna die!"

It is going to be a lonely winter. Ana María has left. One day during one of their chats, Ana's neighbor announced in a tone that left no doubt: "I'm leaving, I'm sick and tired of all this. I'm getting out of Spain. What do you think? I admit that among other things, it has to do with my hopelessly asinine behavior when it comes to the beast." She has gone to England as assistant in a cardiology department. A good job apparently. A newlywed couple has rented her apartment. He is some sort of traveling salesman, or at least it seems that way, judging by the amount of time he spends out of town. She is very young, barely twenty, and already has a baby of around six months.

"You're gonna die, and you're gonna kill me . . ."

One can hear her. One can hear her all day on the other side of the wall. Sometimes she weeps through her soliloquies with the boy, those long slow afternoons consumed inside the empty apartment. She is an odd sort of girl. Always meticulously dressed (each day a new outfit with fashionable shoes and accessories to match), her aged childish face carefully made up. She goes shopping, or for a walk with her kid, all decked out to party, only to lock herself back up in her place. An adolescent with a baby that wails morning, noon, and night. Without

any visitors, without anyone to talk to.

"They just moved to Madrid from La Coruña and they don't have any friends yet," reports the doorwoman, who is in on everything.

The result is that now Ana has to suffer both the tears of the young mother and the screams of the downstairs neighbors, which frighten her more than ever, particularly after last night's scene. Ana cannot help wondering about the strange patterns we are developing for communal living. There is no such thing as a tightly knit community anymore, and now people are subjected to interior pilgrimages, to urban exile. Almost no one lives in the house where they were born; they are scattered around an enormous city that swallows them up and have to struggle to connect with their friends in distant areas. The comforting sense of neighborhood is a thing of the past, and contact with your surroundings is often limited to things like these screams, these crying spells, these weird pantings that permeate the thin walls even as you try to maintain a forced indifference. It is a loneliness with many doors, an urban loneliness of locks and peepholes.

At any rate, it will be a lonely winter. Cecilio is also leaving. He's going to Brazil in two weeks. He won an international architecture contest to build something or other very big in São Paulo. The contract runs for two years. He'll be there at least that long. "I've heard that those Brazilian boys are yummy," he mentions with a playful wink of joy. Julita has already left, but she is not going as far as the others. Her traffic cop was promoted and transferred to a small town outside Madrid, and so she has packed up the kids, wiped her face clean of glitter, and gone to join him at the place they rented in the country. She is working as a secretary for a factory and plans to start a new life there, a relaxed, bucolic existence. "The house is so cheap, Ana, and it even has a nice lot, you'll see how cozy it is." No doubt, it will be cold and lonely this winter.

Furthermore, Ana got up on the wrong side of the bed today. Next to her, all bundled and taking up much more than his corresponding half (she calculates bitchily) lies Gonzalo. A very old friend whom she likes well enough but does not love and with whom she slept last night, who knows why. She had not made love in a while, not since she had decided to do without the hassles of long nights with just any warm body. Nevertheless, last night she had rediscovered old friends in old familiar places, and at that whirlwind pace that evenings sometimes acquire, her body warmed to Gonzalo's advances. She even got to the point of looking at him tenderly. The passing of the mirage, however, gave way to irritation, a gnawing secret irritation at having to share her bed, at the mere impossibility of resting languidly all alone. OK, Anita, she repeated to herself during the interminable night, don't go overboard now, you simply can't throw the guy out at this time, control your aggressiveness, you're being rude and unfair, it's just not decent to make love with him and then send him packing. No matter, her resentment kept on growing. Resentment because in his sleep he rolls over and touches her affectionately. Because his weight prevents her from finding a comfortable position. Because the sound of his deep breathing keeps her awake. Because in the end it seems a monstrosity to have slept with Gonzalo. Ana sighs. She has slept badly, so badly that the music from the neighbors—not screams this time but the thuds of hard rock at three in the morning—found her awake and fuming. Gonzalo was asleep, and Ana felt her fury grow. Finally she got up, threw on a robe, went down to the second floor muttering to herself on the way, "I've had it, when they're not thrashing each other about, they're shaking the building with their music." She rang the bell, heard a rustle on the other side of the door, and finally it swung open. It was not the boy with the innocent smile, purported torturer of helpless women; it was not the girl with the faded eyes, nor the dark one with the wild curls. It was a new girl that Ana did not know, a long-haired blond wearing velvet pants and a vest. "Yes?" she said. "I'm your upstairs neighbor. Excuse me, but could you turn down the music a bit?" And as she was

enough, she enjoyed making love with him last night. At this thought, Ana huffs with irritated gloom. She has noticed that when she is in love with her partner, it is much more difficult for her to have an orgasm. She never had one with José María. It was only afterward, when she began to forget him, that sex with him became less tense, more focused. She usually gets along better sexually with men with whom she is merely friends and whom she is, therefore, betraying. Ana also betrays the men she loves deeply. Of course she gets real pleasure from making love with them, but she never reaches orgasm. She fakes it. We are all such lousy fucks.

"Do you want to know something?" she blurts out loud. "I don't think orgasm is as important as it's cracked up to be."

Gonzalo gapes at her, a dripping roll in midair halfway between the coffee cup and his mouth.

"What was that?"

"It's all wrong, this obsession with orgasm," explains Ana, infuriated now. "We've mistaken orgasm for sex when it's only a small part of it." She sighs, reflects for a minute: "Part of the blame lies with Henry Miller and his insatiable women and also with Wilhelm Reich and his damned orgone theory."

"Fine," Gonzalo replies, somewhat regaining his composure. "I'm not sure I catch all the subtleties of what you're getting at, but in any case I don't think that you can compare Reich with that idiot Henry Miller."

"What I'm trying to say is that we give such disproportionate importance to orgasm that lovemaking is mostly an anxious race to the finish . . . I think that is peculiar to Western cultures . . . I've heard that the Chinese, for instance, have a very different approach. According to the Tao, both pleasure and health derive from holding back and controlling oneself."

"Frankly, I don't find that a very appealing notion."

They both laugh.

"Neither do I, but then, I'm not Chinese . . . but I do mean it, without going to such extremes, we are slaves to the myth of orgasm. And I agree with your appreciation of Reich, he's a solid writer. But I'm very disturbed by the fact that he had to tie all his good discoveries to the supremacy of orgasms."

"Perhaps it's his followers who make such a fuss about it . . ."

"May well be . . ."

The tyrannical orgasm. Yes, that's just it, Ana is convinced. Once again, it is a matter of stereotypes: men have to be potent, women insatiable. Lovers do not make love, do not feel each other, do not play around. They embark, full of fear and anticipated frustration, on a feverish race toward orgasm. If she doesn't have one, she feels weird and inadequate. And if he doesn't give it to her, he feels clumsy, defeated, less than manly. So Ana fakes it—like millions of women, she fakes it, and no one dares to tell the truth, everyone is so caught up in the prescribed role of the lover. With casual friends with whom there is not so much at stake, sex is a lot easier, because she can afford to be herself. But with the ones she loves Ana wants to be up to the demands of her part, and fearing disappointment for both she fakes, acts out, invents an orgasm to avoid worrying her partner, or inhibiting him, and to give an air of triumph to the battle.

Because that kind of sex is a battle. It's codified, structured, tied to norms and curtsies; it is a battle between two people, both in search of the thousand legendary orgasms invented by Henry Miller. It is a narrow, anxious kind of sex without room for fantasy, laughter, sensuality, complicity, healthy obscenity, play. And words.

"Why don't you ever talk during sex?" Ana's words shoot out of her mouth.

"Who, me?"

"All you men . . ."

Ana is thinking about how Spanish men never talk during lovemaking. They are so fully concentrated on their empty gestures—always haunted by the ghost of failure—that they are incapable of verbalizing all the images that are surely running through their minds. In general they don't moan, don't express their pleasure, don't allow themselves to be moved. They are like scarabs busily turning their ball, locked within themselves, taciturn, obsessed. Where are they in the meantime, what oppressive walls keep them hidden from view? In the end they come, and in many cases this is also imperceptible save for a slightly tighter hug, or to the contrary, a strange immobility. Precious little. They come as if into themselves, with their emotions perfectly under control. At times in their orgasms there is more relief at "having arrived" than pleasure in the act itself. Ana believes there is something very wrong in all of this. That she is not only a victim but also an accomplice. That she still fakes it out of fear of not measuring up to male standards, to that macho creed that enslaves both men and women today. Her fear of disappointing, of being less than the classic lover, makes her give repeat performances which keep the show going. We are chained to our roles and live out our stereotypes. Elena says something of the sort in her essay "Odd and Even": There is one role for the man and another for the woman; one for old people, one for the young. There is one for fathers and one for sons, one for traditional and one for liberated women, one for the deranged and one for the sane, one for the successful, one for the defeated. They are all rigid characters, empty and unreal, mere distorted images of humankind.

They are quietly smoking a cigarette after breakfast when a sharp, tearful wail makes its way through the walls. "What on earth was that?" Gonzalo asks in amazement. "Oh, just the neighbors, they're kind of berserk and they beat up on each other," Ana explains as she feels her soul shrivel when faced with this early morning violence.

"Mama, what is that?"

Curro has just awakened and is calling from his room. The screams always scare him. "Nothing, sweetheart, the neighbors are fooling around." She dresses him to the rhythm of the blows, and finally there is a long moan, a sort of last desolate growl that reverberates like a death rattle. Then there is silence. One day we'll find out that one of them has been murdered, Ana reflects somberly, as she recalls the puffy abused face of the blond. She is overcome with panic; it must be a cult of some sort, all of them deranged. If I intervene or complain, they may harm me or Curro.

"Come eat some breakfast, babe, you have to come with me to the office."

Curro walks into the living room and stops in his tracks to stare at Gonzalo, his mouth tightening into a suspicious and unfriendly frown. In the end, ignoring Gonzalo's cheerful greetings, Curro turns to Ana and asks point-blank:

"Where did he sleep?"

His tense and accusing finger is directed at Gonzalo.

"I don't know," Ana answers with a smile. "I imagine he slept in his house. He just walked in to have breakfast with us. Didn't you hear the door?"

(It is impossible that Curro could've heard him last night. He was sound asleep when we arrived, I paid the sitter and we went straight to my room. This kid is unbelievable; no matter how hard I try to hide my dealings with men from him, he's got a sixth sense for these things.)

The boy stares at her in silence, his dark eyes heavy with misgivings. Finally he says: "He slept with you, and I don't want him to. I don't, I don't."

Gonzalo turns pale, and Ana weaves together a host of non-sensical, incoherent explanations. The ringing telephone puts an end to this embarrassing scene.

"Hello."

"Ana. It's José María."

She is surprised and cannot think of anything to say.

"Oh."

"There's no way to get through to you. I've called a bunch of times but you're never there. And you don't bother to call me back lately . . ."

The plaintive tone of this last sentence irritates Ana. It's so late, José

María, she thinks to herself, it's so late, you are such an ass, such a jerk, such a coward. Aloud she only replies:

"If you feel like it we can have dinner tonight. Or, actually, rather not tonight. I went out yesterday and I want to stay home with Curro. How 'bout tomorrow night?"

On her way to the office she feels that the dark winter clouds are a foreboding presence, intimations of disaster. Curro is aloof; there is a biting wind and Ana is always frightened, always wary, of its desolate, inhuman hissing. Agreeing to see José María was a coldly premeditated decision. She wants to have him seated across from her so she can hurt him. She wants to ask him the point of his frequent calls, the meaning of his loving, imploring tone just now, the use of trying to revive an affair that withered long ago. It is her night for revenge. You are a creep, I'll tell him, coming around playing at love. It's much too late. And with a ferocity that she did not know herself capable of, she wishes to break his unflappable self-assurance, wreck his life, make him cry.

"Hi, love, I'm leaving the *News*." There is no doubt about it, Mateo is a bit high: he slurs his *l*'s slightly, his eyes have an unusual glint, and his cheeks glow from alcohol and excitement. On his desk are several empty bottles of champagne next to a pile of used paper cups, the remnants of a toast to his imminent departure.

"Are you kidding . . ."

"Nope, I mean it. I'm the new editor of the *Northern Herald* in San Sebastián."

"Wow . . ."

Ana is sorry to see Mateo leave, in spite of his Machiavellian habit of agreeing to everything and doing as he pleases, in spite of his tendency to load her with work and abuse her with a gentle hand. In spite of all that, Mateo is one of the few people there capable of showing affection and respect for others. She has grown accustomed to him.

"Well, I'm sorry to see you go, of course, but I'm delighted that you have such a wonderful opportunity."

"I'm ecstatic . . . this is such a madhouse, not only because of all the bureaucracy but now, with Ramses, our hands are really tied. You should've seen his face when I told him."

"Whose?"

"Ramses, who else? His hair got ruffled with the shock. Don't do it, man, this is a real blow, he said. Some bastard, after having me here for fifteen years working like a dog. By the way, you got a phone call, I took the message down on that piece of paper."

Yes, there is no doubt that Mateo is drunk, otherwise he would not have dared to say those things out loud. The message was from Elena: Javier was already home, so not to bother to stop by the hospital. Fine. She remembers with a shudder that they removed a testicle and slit him wide open to take out a whole set of lymph nodes. A new method to prevent metastasis, or so they claim. But there are no guarantees, everything is experimental when it comes to cancer. He is on a strict protocol, brutal treatments that cause racking pain and nausea while his hair, his long beautiful locks, fall out in dead clumps. Two years. If he survives two years without a relapse—and he's merely thirty-two—perhaps he can make it. The younger you are, the fiercer the onslaught of cancer. The more alive you are, the greedier is that quiet, invasive tumor. Each day, every hour, there are new cases, close calls, different victims, as if the disease were spreading and winning the battle. A disease that eats your insides and feeds on our absurd life-style: cigarettes, plastics, canned food. We are slowly committing suicide.

"Is this the main desk of the *Daily News*?"

"Yes," Ana says, reluctantly answering the phone.

"Look, I'm calling from the Grandview subdivision again. I know you must be sick of hearing from us so often, but there's another corpse in our yard and we're fed up . . ."

"I beg your pardon?"

"Another corpse, this time it's a Chinese man, and it's been there

ing, stand a police car and a fire truck, their metallic lights turning in the frozen dusk. On the street a crowd is gathered: some neighbors, the man from the corner newspaper stand, Doña Pura, the woman from the bakery shop. Ana is certain that finally something drastic has happened, that one of the downstairs tenants has been killed, perhaps the dark one beaten to death with her frizzy hair caked in blood from the gash on her head. Or the one with the faded eyes now definitely empty, asphyxiated by some hands that have left purplish marks around her neck. Or last night's blond, stabbed to death in the bathtub. Ana approaches the throng taking the child by the hand, don't get away from me. The doorwoman is relating the details at the top of her lungs to a select few: ". . . and the firemen had to knock down the door . . ." At that moment the ambulance arrives howling. "Let us through, let us through," the men with the stretcher demand. People back off in expectant, murmuring waves. Doña Pura inquires, "But is she dead?" And the doorwoman answers, "Yes, totally dead, she must have died hours ago, that's what they said." "Good heavens, good heavens," neighboring women are heard to say. "How awful," another one adds, "I saw her just yesterday or was it the day before?" Ana, horrified, tightens her grip on Curro's hand, "Mama, you're hurting me." She draws nearer to ask, "How did she die?" "No one knows for sure, she must have fallen down or had an attack or maybe it was just old age." "My God, to die like that, just like a dog," Doña Pura mutters. "What do you mean 'old age'?" Ana asks. "Just who died?" The neighbors interrupt each other, all eager to explain the tragedy. It was Doña Engracia, the little old lady on the ground floor. Didn't you know her? Yes, of course, the wispy one who always wore black. Get it now? They discovered her so soon because the mailman brought her retirement check today, and she didn't pick it up. She could barely walk and spent her days cooped up inside. The doorwoman called the police. Ana notices that the mysterious neighbor and the blond with the bruised face have joined the crowd, and he has his arm around her frail shoulders. Anyway, when they knocked the door down they found Doña Engracia in the dark dining room jammed with old, damp furniture. She was on the floor like a crumpled mourning rag. Her left hand still clung to the leg of that heavy widow's armchair, and her nails had peeled off the varnish and torn the upholstery in her efforts to reach the door.

Thirteen

"Anything wrong with you?"

It sounds more like an accusation than a question. José María and Ana are sitting in a tiny neighborhood restaurant that they have frequented for years. She has held out through the soup and part of the main course but finally blurts out across her half-eaten steak:

"Anything wrong with you?"

She tries to capture in one sentence all the interminable hours waiting by the telephone, all her long repressed yearnings, all the unsaid words that she has stored for ten years.

"With me? Nothing."

José María seems surprised by the tone of Ana's voice. Their relationship has always been civilized, upbeat and teasing, an aloof and witty relationship that made serious and intimate talk seem in bad taste.

"With you. With you."

This time Ana is being deadly serious, surprisingly serious, ridiculously serious. The many roles that she has assumed over the years have become a burden, and Ana feels naked talking to José María without her habitual laughter as a smiling shield.

"Lately all you do is call and, well, you blame me for never calling you, for not taking the initiative. Haven't you caught on yet? For years we've only seen one another when it suited you. We had a tacit agreement. And now, and only now, it looks like you're unhappy with the whole situation. What kind of game are you playing?"

"Hey, wait a second, what's with you tonight?"

José María bursts out laughing and looks at Ana with a bemused expression of surprise. "Let's start all over," he suggests. "Let's pretend we've just sat down and I asked you what's the matter. From the way you're acting, it seems the question would be more appropriate coming from me, don't you think?"

"Don't laugh. I'm sick and tired of our being clever and witty with one another. For years we haven't had a single serious conversation. You have an ingrained fear of committing your feelings to words."

"Ana, I don't know what you're talking about." José María is still smiling but guardedly now, like someone who is venturing into unknown territory. "Besides, you're blaming me for something we both did. What I mean is . . . if I've been so clever and witty with you, which I happen to doubt, you've been playing the same game with me, right?"

"Of course. That's because when we first met, I tried to have a serious conversation with you and you laughed at me. Well, after a couple of times I stopped. I catch on quick, you know."

There is a long silence. José María is thrown off guard. Ana nervously crushes bread crumbs against the table. "We've had an idiotic and one-sided relationship," she says at last. "You've always known how much I loved you, and I . . . and I . . ."

"I'm not so sure about that," he cuts in, "it's just not true. I've not always known."

"What do you mean you haven't? How can you say that?" Ana is fuming, boiling over with rage. "I was just a kid, you were living with a woman, I was free, and I wanted to live with you. I told you. I told you so many times."

"No. You didn't."

"Yes, I did! Listen (now I'm going to launch into a long and tedious argument, the kind old married couples get into. I'll tally up all the past hurts and resentments you've long forgotten—the dates you forgot to keep, the times you slighted me, the year you refused to . . . how you paid no attention when . . .), listen. Don't you remember those first weeks we spent together? Remember when you went to meet your girlfriend in Barcelona? I told you. I told you I'd see you whenever you called. I couldn't call you because you were the one who was always so busy, but I told you I'd see you whenever you called. And I never let you down, never, for years. Don't forget it."

"I'm telling you that it wasn't so clear to me."

"What do you mean, it wasn't! What more could I have done? José María, this is an idiotic conversation. If, as you say, it wasn't clear before, let me make myself perfectly clear now. I loved you more than any other man. I loved you for years and years. I missed you so much . . . you can't imagine how much. But not anymore. You can't hurt me anymore. I don't love you anymore. You can't cause me any more pain. And now—what a coincidence!—you call me every day."

By now Ana has lost all control. She despises him and wants to make sure that he knows.

"For years I thought you were such a strong man—so calm and stable. Of course, I was pretty young and you were an adult. Now I know that you go through life pretending to be Superman. Well, that's a luxury you pay dearly for . . . do you know that in all the time we've known each other you've never once confided in me? Never. Not once. Not one doubt, not one worry, not one weakness. You make yourself out to be the perfect man. No crises, no depressions, no hangups . . . you amaze me."

José María raises his sad brown eyes, just like a faithful dog, and answers slowly. "I didn't tell you any of my problems because I was afraid I'd bore you with them. The fact is, we saw each other so rarely that I didn't want to be a drag . . ."

Ana is too furious to pay attention to what he is saying, yet she feels a knot in the pit of her stomach as he speaks. It is as if an alarm has gone off in the distance, yet she refuses to heed the warning now that she is relishing her sweet revenge.

"Do you know what it's like to keep on loving a person who never responds," she asks him, "without ever knowing what you mean to him? Well, that's exactly what's happening right now. I've just told you that you were the man that I've loved the most in my life, and you still don't answer. You don't say a word. You're like a wall to me, a mirror that reflects my own image."

"All right, fine. Listen. I'll tell you." José María hesitates. It is a struggle for him to find the right words. "Now that you've asked, I'll tell you. It's just that . . . well, for all these years I've thought of you as . . . I've sort of idealized you. I don't know if . . . I mean, I thought . . . especially in times of crisis that with you . . . yes, that you and I could have a satisfying relationship. I thought that some day we'd do it, that some day we'd try it, when we were both free, when the right occasion came up . . . because I was never so sure that you wanted to live with me. No matter what you say now, I never believed it."

What a strange sensation! It is as if all her tendons had suddenly relaxed, and her arms and legs lost all their strength. Her back and shoulders slump. Ana feels her aggression melt away as she hears José María's words. Something snaps inside and condenses her hatred into tears, a steady stream that drenches what's left of the steak and embarrasses José María.

"Oh . . . please don't, you make me feel terrible." It is the first time he has seen her cry.

So everything is crystal clear. José María is really an insecure and affectionate man, not that aloof and stable person she thought she knew. His toughness was nothing but an outer shell. As for herself, ah, for years she played the part of the hard and independent woman; she played it so well that she scared him to death. With a sudden rush of understanding, Ana sees through their ten years of misencounters and lies and realizes how little they truly know one another after such a long time. Like marionettes, they pulled their own strings and deceived each other. She feels that they have robbed themselves of an irreplaceable part of their lives.

"It's too late," Ana snivels, vaguely aware that she is making a scene in the old restaurant, "and besides, these things leave their mark. They scar you for life."

It is midnight, closing time, and the restaurant lights are turned down. They leave, Ana's cheeks still wet with memories. Outside, an ice storm is raging, and the parked cars are covered with slush.

"This blows my mind." José María's voice sounds upbeat but forced. "You start into me with 'what's wrong with you' and you end up bawling." Ana smiles weakly through her tears. They get to his car and climb in. "Shall we go to your place?" Ana would prefer to go home alone, fervently wishing to put an end to their talk, to lock herself up in her gloom, and to sleep. She is so tired. But her tears are too fresh, and there is too little time to patch things up. It's clear that he will take her home, that he will go inside and want to make love. They drive through the deserted city streets in the freezing rain. There are hardly any cars and no pedestrians, only a youngish couple in brightly colored sweatsuits—his green, hers red—jogging along the empty pavement. Columns of vapor are rising from their noses, and between their legs trots a yapping fox terrier that tries to nip the ankles of his owners as he keeps pace.

He jokes. José María keeps up his tender, affectionate, and timid banter. Between jokes he begins to kiss her and, once in her apartment, to help her undress. Ana feels no desire, but her hatred has completely disappeared, and she no longer wants to hurt him. She knows that her tears have had their effect. He makes love to her differently—he kisses her neck, he caresses her, he is the tender lover that Ana had always wanted him to be. "Your skin is so soft," he whispers, and this awakens in her the sharp pain of their irreversibly mistimed love. Not too eagerly, she fakes an orgasm, feeling old and far removed. At some point Ana notices amid the curls of José María's pubic hair the first few strands of gray.

Fourteen

"You're all a bunch of pricks!"

Ana is furious. She is so furious that she is at a loss for words, so furious that she cannot assume a serene and composed demeanor. She is choking on her own rage, with full knowledge—intuition nurtured by experience—that she is on the brink of defeat.

"You're a bunch of fucking pricks."

Her tears well up inside and she feels alone and helpless. These are the feelings that she most hates and despises in herself, as if they were the atavistic remnants of an alien self, a creature from an effeminate culture that she rejects. "They wouldn't dare do this to a man," she seethes. "If they did, he would stir up a scandal that would leave them all shaking in their boots." But Ana knows that her outburst will only provoke a paternal and consoling gesture from Mateo, a well-intended and totally ineffective pat on her back as he says, "Calm down, love, don't get upset." Nothing will change, and her anger will have been wasted.

"Calm down, love, don't get so upset."

“Why shouldn’t I? I’ve been with this fucking firm for two years, and you’ve used me as a pawn. I work harder than anyone on the editorial staff, I get stuck with all the drudge work, I’m the one you call on Sunday night to say that some article has been scrapped and I have to come up with a new one by Monday noon, the paper must go out, blah, blah, blah. And all for pennies, I’m not even on salary, I don’t even get paid for the articles that you assign and then decide not to print. Let’s face it, you’ve got me pegged as the slave and the dummy, and when I protest, you say, ‘Love, you’re indispensable, next year we’ll make you permanent.’ Ha! What a joke . . . I’m such a fool.”

It has been barely half an hour since Domingo, the managing editor, blushing and nervously cracking his knuckles, told Ana: “Look, it’s impossible for the time being. Now don’t worry, we’re working on it, we’ll come up with something, we’ll do our best to bring you on full time.” Ana thinks about Curro, how he’ll be starting school this year, how each day it’s harder to make ends meet . . . and grimaces bitterly to herself. Being a single mother is a real feat: you have all the responsibilities of the head of the family and none of the privileges. It was the same when she lost her job at the bank for being pregnant. The head of personnel called her into his office. He was cunning and ambitious and ultraconservative, a member of the *Opus Dei.* His pasty smooth skin looked like it had been dusted with talcum powder. “You do understand, Ana,” he said in an unctuous voice, “you do see that you cannot continue working here. Of course, we have no intention of throwing you out on the street. You’ll get your severance pay, enough to carry you through until your child is born, and of course the bank will cover the hospital costs and medical expenses. But we don’t want you back here.” (He lowered his voice in a humiliating aside: “You’re already beginning to show.”) “You’ll have time later to find another job. With your skills, it won’t be hard.” Ana knew enough to bite her lip, to control herself, not to give him the thanks he expected for his niggardly offer. He, of course, had seven or eight or nine kids, a whole passel of legitimate children, sanctimoniously conceived in a joyless state of grace.

"Look here, Ana, I stuck up for you, I insisted that they make you full time, you have my word," Mateo is saying, "and besides, here you are, number one on the list, the next one to be brought on board and as soon as possible, don't you doubt it for a second. It's just that the higher-ups got it in their head to hire Paco Alamo from the *Madrid Daily News*. They wanted a specialist in national politics."

"Of course. And a woman can only specialize in fillers."

"It's not that, it's not that at all, cutie. You know how they are, they have no notion of good journalism, they had their sights set on taking over the guy's paper, and that's how they did it."

"And what about the other two new guys?"

"Well, Ascano is a personal friend of Ramses, and José Luis is Domingo's pal."

(And the bastard fidgeted with his hands and looked so forlorn while he gave her the bad news that Ana felt the urge to console him.)

"But don't you worry, Domingo has assured me that they'll write you up a set monthly contract. Before I leave here, I'll make sure they sign it."

Promises, promises. Mateo always makes promises, perhaps even intending to follow through. But then the bureaucratic monster of the *News* swallows him up, chews him to shreds, and spits him out.

"Cheer up, gorgeous. Put all this out of your mind and let's go party. Tonight's the office Christmas bash, the one they throw every year at Boccaccio's. You'll see, a couple of drinks and you'll snap right out of it."

"I don't drink."

"OK, kid, then a Coca-Cola."

The place is overflowing with guests who must perform difficult gymnastic exercises just to squeeze through the tightly packed crowd without spilling their drinks or burning anyone with their cigarettes.

Ana hates these noisy parties where she feels out of place, but she has a motive for showing up tonight: she has come hoping to meet Soto Amón. Of course he'll be there, she is sure of it. Ana wants him more than ever. For the past two weeks, ever since her spat with José María, she has been feeling dejected and empty. Behind her is a failure; ahead an impossible and idiotic make-believe romance. In spite of everything, Ana has been so overcome with longing for the unreachable Soto Amón that she wastes all sorts of energy outlining their imaginary first encounter—what he will say, how she will answer, how he will lavish his attention and affection on her. And realizing with some astonishment that she has never been romantically involved with a man who wears a tie, she delights in trying to solve this little problem: how to undress him, how to loosen the knot of his perfectly squared tie.

"Well, Mateo!"

It is Soto Amón, drink in hand, a hyper and flushed Soto Amón.

"Am I glad to see you. I can't put up with these jerks any longer. The old guard on the Board of Directors is here campaigning. They want the *Weekly News* to support Fraga and the ultra-right in the next elections. They're nuts."

He is a funny, extroverted, and very human Soto Amón tonight. Perhaps the cocktails have loosened the bonds of shyness that Ana either intuits or attributes to him. Perhaps being away from the confines of the office has diluted his rigid sense of power into a more egalitarian mold.

"Do you know Ana Antón? She works for us . . . well, I should say for you, since I . . ." says Mateo feistily.

"We've seen one another at the office often enough. And of course I've read her . . ."

Ana wants to believe that his wide grin and friendly words are sincere, and she reels from the combination of the stifling heat, the excitement of the evening, and his presence. She notices that her heart is pounding.

They exchange small talk on neutral topics, straining to be heard over the music and the noise. Ana feels dull and awkward; she is almost speechless. Although at other times she can be clever, or at least witty, situations like this intimidate her and her mind snaps shut. She feels like a schoolgirl at her first teenage party.

"Let's get out of here," says Soto Amón abruptly. "I know a quiet place. We have to celebrate your farewell, Mateo."

One round, two rounds, three rounds in a nearby pub, and Mateo has to prop his elbow against the posh leather bar to continue the story of his life with all its lurid details. His virginal visit to a brothel at age sixteen, the flowered wallpaper, the red neon light, the madam with the washbasin. Soto Amón laughs. He also has drunk a lot but looks as if he can hold it.

"Shall we have dinner?" he finally asks, and Ana feels cold sweat trickling down her neck.

"Not me, not me. I can't, sorry, I can't. Seriously." Mateo is slurring his words. "I promised my wife I'd take her to the theater . . . damn, what time is it? I gotta run. No, no, the last round's on me," he insists as Soto Amón reaches for the tab, and with a shaky hand sprinkles the bar with hundred-peseta bills. He plants big wet kisses on Ana's cheek, thumps Eduardo on the back, and for a moment looks as if he is going to kiss him too. He gets as far as the door, then turns for one more grandiose goodbye before finally leaving.

"Well, now," Soto Amón flashes Ana a dazzling smile. "You're not going to slip away from me, are you? I know just the place for dinner." He takes her by the arm and whisks her out the door.

The restaurant is intimate, romantic, and expensive. Ana ordered fish but has hardly touched it. She cannot force herself to swallow a bite. Across the table Eduardo wolfs down his food and somehow manages to chew out of one side of his mouth and talk out of the other.

"So you have a son."

"That's right. Curro is almost . . ."

"I have three myself, you know. All grown by now, of course."

Soto Amón is used to butting in, to silencing others, and seems to have lost the ability to listen.

"You have no idea how lucky you are. You're young, attractive, bright . . . you have your son and you're not tied down to anyone . . . or are you?" His seemingly casual question irritates Ana, who sees it as a clumsy way to find out if she has a husband or a boyfriend, or is up for grabs.

"I'm not."

"Well, isn't that marvelous. You have your entire life ahead of you. On the other hand, I . . ." He lets out a weary sigh.

Ana starts to dread hearing another caged-bird tale about a marriage on the rocks: We were married young . . . I was just a kid. My wife and I don't get along, we're both miserable. The burden of success . . . so lonely at the top . . . She folds the napkin on her lap and keeps her fingers crossed: Dear God, don't let him dare talk like that. Please, please, make him wise up.

"I got married when I was barely twenty, like just about everyone of my generation. I was just a silly kid. Needless to say, after twenty years of marriage there's nothing left. It's doubly true in a case like mine. I know, you're going to tell me that I could've gotten a legal separation. It's not that easy, you know, especially if you have children. When they're young, they tie you down. Later, after they've grown up, you're already caught in the trap, safely stuck in the rut. I must admit that my situation is rather convenient, even if it's not exactly noble. What I mean is . . . I provide her with a name, a certain status, a mink coat . . . and she provides me with the necessary accoutrements and the official comforts of hearth and home. What can I say? My wife suits my position. She is elegant, sophisticated, and not totally brainless . . . she majored in literature in college. Ours is a marriage of convenience, clear and simple. She goes her way and I go mine."

"Mostly you go yours." Ana snaps at him and immediately feels like biting her tongue.

“Perhaps you’re right, mostly I go mine. But she has the same options to do whatever she pleases. She just doesn’t want them. For example, I’d be delighted if she took a lover . . . as long as she was discreet. Like me. I guess I must seem jaded. And I suppose I am somewhat. But I’ve paid dearly for it.”

At this point, Eduardo puts on the desolate expression of one who bears his load in silence.

“I’m not close to my children. They do their own thing. My wife and I haven’t talked in years. At the *Weekly News*—there’s no use mentioning it—I’m the boss and that’s always a lonely job. Power has its rewards, of course. I’m not going to make myself out to be the victim, but still . . .”

And his entire face contorts into a visual contradiction of his words . . . yes, into the face of the victim, the long-suffering victim resigned to his fate. Then he raises his eyes and gives her an embarrassed but splendid smile:

“I don’t know why I’m telling you all this.”

Silence.

“It’s been so long since I’ve really talked to anyone, it feels like I’ve known you for years.”

Anguish. Ana is in anguish hearing such clichés, recognizing the obligatory pose that accompanies each phrase—the timed smile, the intimate tone, the sigh. Her stomach hurts, her cheeks burn, her hands sweat. He is casting his net and crudely pulling it in. In spite of her premonition, her intuitive knowledge of the true Soto Amón, Ana knows that she will end up going to bed with him, carried away by the inertia of one year of longing, and clinging to the slim hope that he might yet prove to be different.

“Don’t mind the place, it’s a mess. Well now . . .”

He is pouring another scotch. “Are you sure you don’t want one?” He gets some ice from a small refrigerator built into the wall. Everything is plastic and white formica in this pretentiously modern bachelor pad in the heart of Madrid, and the entrance, with direct access from the garage, is so discreet. Music provides a neutral and impersonal backdrop. It is bland and colorless. He draws close, kisses her quickly and competently, and then begins to undress.

(With a doomed sense of certainty, Ana foresees how their evening will develop. He'll undress me with expert and aloof hands. We'll try a few meaningless embraces, we'll have impersonal sex without so much as saying a word. He'll have an orgasm without me—without hugging me, without seeing me, without remembering who I am. There will be a discreet and minimally friendly moment of respite, and immediately afterward the glance at the clock—sorry, I've gotta go, it's part of the deal with my wife—and we'll quickly and silently get dressed, the apartment will seem uglier by the minute, maybe I'll put the dirty glass and ashtrays in the sink out of an automatic female response. Leave it, he'll insist, the cleaning woman is coming in the morning. We'll go down to the street, he'll act tough, cold, and aloof. Do you mind if I hail you a cab? I'm really late, he might even add. I'll feel ridiculous, disappointed, and I'll say that no it doesn't matter, knowing full well that he's not driving me home only because he wants to keep a clear distance, so it doesn't go to my head, so I don't get any ideas, in order to show me that what we did holds absolutely no meaning.)

The charade unfolds with a shocking resemblance to her premonition (what am I doing here with this stranger?): they have hushed and hollow sex (what an absurd situation, thoroughly, totally absurd); the air is charged with silence (it's as if I were looking at myself from afar—far away from reality, from him, from everything); "I'm sorry but it's awfully late, we better go," he says at last (one whole year winds up like this, if he only knew), "leave it, Ana, leave everything as it is, a maid comes in every day to straighten things up."

"Don't drive me home. I'll take a taxi."

They are in the entrance; he looks surprised and relieved: "I'd really appreciate it, because . . . are you sure you don't mind?" "No, not at all, in fact I'd much rather." Ana answers matter-of-factly, but she can see in his eyes that his relief has given way to a shadow of doubt, a glimmer of suspicion. "Are you positive you don't want me to take you home?" He is now insistent, suddenly solicitous, paying strict attention to her for the first time in the entire evening. (I can't believe it—is it possible that one little rise out of me can affect him so much, can make him insecure and perhaps even deflate his fragile male ego? Can this powerful, successful man be afraid that he may have failed me as a lover? Can he be that immature?) "Positive," Ana replies. Eduardo stares at her for a few moments. He seems uncomfortable and disconcerted. "Are you sure you're all right?" he finally asks, hiding the anxious tone of his voice behind a mask of paternalism. Ana suddenly feels the irrepressible urge to laugh hysterically. She manages to answer between fits of laughter, "I'm just fine, better than ever. And you?" She gives him a light kiss on the cheek, turns away, and walks along the empty street, leaving Soto Amón glued to the sidewalk, staring after her.

Now she has to crisscross Madrid, hideously ugly at this hour of the morning, pick up Curro at his grandparents' house: Do you know what time it is? Now the boy will wake up. Shame on you. Curro whimpers half-asleep with his arms around his mother's neck—it's all right, love, it's all right—and the worst is still to come, her most difficult ordeal. She still has to face the brazen neon light in the elevator, the unrepentant mirror that reflects defeat in the huge bags under the eyes, the late-night pallor of the cheeks, and the thirty years that are beginning to furrow down her face. She thinks about Cecilio in far-off Brazil, flaunting loves that he too knows are false. Her apartment is colder and more lonely than ever, two blankets for the boy's bed—sleep, love, sleep. When Curro, his face still red from crying, starts breathing softly and evenly, there wells up inside Ana a rare and intense pride, a calm conviction that in this chess game of losers those who lose the most are the ones like Soto Amón who do not even play. Of all those feverish months she laments only the utter waste of imagination and tenderness.

Of the entire evening's misadventure her sole regret is that Soto Amón loosened his own tie in an automatic and well-practiced act of self-sufficiency, a cruel display of power. But, who knows? With a caustic smile, she thinks this might make a fine opening for the book that she now is sure to write. It will no longer be the bitter *Ana's Book* but rather a journal, a chronicle of the absence of love in daily life, bearing the rubric of an ordinary silk tie undone by routine and boredom.

Other volumes in the European Women Writers Series include:

Artemisia
By Anna Banti
Translated by Shirley D'Ardia Caracciolo

Bitter Healing
German Women Writers from 1700 to 1830
An Anthology
Edited by Jeannine Blackwell and Susanne Zantop

The Book of Promethea
By Hélène Cixous
Translated by Betsy Wing

Maria Zef
By Paola Drigo
Translated by
Blossom Steinberg Kirschenbaum

Woman to Woman
By Marguerite Duras and Xavière Gauthier
Translated by Katherine A. Jensen

The Tongue Snatchers
By Claudine Herrmann
Translated by Nancy Kline

Mother Death
By Jeanne Hyvrard
Translated by Laurie Edson

The House of Childhood
By Marie Luise Kaschnitz
Translated by Anni Whissen

The Panther Woman
Five Tales from the Cassette Recorder
By Sarah Kirsch
Translated by Marion Faber

On Our Own Behalf
Women's Tales from Catalonia
Edited by Kathleen McNerney

The Delta Function
By Rosa Montero
Translated by Kari A. Easton and Yolanda Molina Gavilán

Music from a Blue Well
By Torborg Nedreaas
Translated by Bibbi Lee

Nothing Grows by Moonlight
By Torborg Nedreaas
Translated by Bibbi Lee

Why Is There Salt in the Sea?
By Brigitte Schwaiger
Translated by Sieglinde Lug

The Same Sea As Every Summer
By Esther Tusquets
Translated by Margaret E. W. Jones